Derborence

Derborence

by

Charles Ferdinand Ramuz

Translated by

Laura Spinney

Skomlin
House of Memory

Skomlin
House of Memory and Imagination
For more information visit *www.skomlin.com*

A Skomlin Book
London, Melbourne, New York

First published in Switzerland in 1934
English translation by Laura Spinney © 2018
Foreword by Laura Spinney © 2018
Afterword by Laura Spinney © 2018

This edition © Skomlin, 2018

ISBN: 978-1-7892658-1-1 *(paperback)*
ISBN: 978-0-6482521-8-4 *(eBook)*

The paper used in this publication meets the minimum requirements of ANSI/NISO Z39.48-1992 (R1997) (Permanence of Paper). The paper used in this book is from responsibly managed forests. Printed in the United States of America, the United Kingdom and Australia by Lightning Source, Inc.

Foreword

I arrived in Switzerland in a blizzard. It was 2009, my husband had accepted a post in Lausanne, on the northern shore of Lake Geneva, and I had followed him. Neither the lake nor the Alps on the far shore – the French shore – were visible that evening, but when I woke the next morning there they were, very still, very close. Over the next few days they receded, closed in, receded again. At times I could make out the ripples on the water, or the crevices in the rock; at others those surfaces appeared smooth. After four full seasons in my new home I no longer had faith in my ability to judge distance. As anyone who has lived in that part of the world will tell you, something strange happens to perspective there. The light, including the moonlight, conspires with the terrain to transform it in a continual process of renewal. Having been reared in tamer landscapes, I found it unsettling. Sometimes it was my paradise, sometimes my prison.

One day a colleague of my husband's came to dinner and brought *Derborence*, and reading it had much the same effect on me as that first encounter with the mountains, because the author, Charles Ferdinand Ramuz – who grew up in the same part of Switzerland – took that oddly elastic perspective and wove it into his fiction. He fitted an entire universe between that lake and those mountains, and then he examined that universe from every possible vantage point: yours, mine, ours, theirs; from inside, from outside, from the bottom of a dank gorge, through the beady eye of an eagle soaring overhead. He shifted between them fluidly and without warning, making you question things you had taken for granted, things you thought were solid. To read his books is to understand that they could only have been written in that place, but that they explain much more than that place. Six years after arriving in Switzerland I left again, but now, wherever I go, Ramuz comes with me.

Laura Spinney

PART ONE

I

…A shepherd who had vanished and whom everyone thought dead, spent several months buried inside a mountain chalet, surviving on bread and cheese…

GEOGRAPHICAL DICTIONARY

In his right hand he held a sort of long stick, blackened at the end, that he thrust every now and then into the fire. The other hand rested on his left thigh.

It was the twenty-second of June, about nine in the evening.

He stoked the fire with his wand of sparks. They clung to the soot-covered wall, shining like stars in a black sky.

For an instant, during which he held his poker still, you saw him better, Séraphin. You saw the man opposite him too, a much younger man, his elbows resting likewise on his raised knees, his head hanging.

"So that's it," said Séraphin, the elder of the two. "You're bored."

He looked at Antoine and smiled into his white beard.

"We haven't even been up here that long."

They had come up around the fifteenth of June, with the people from Aïre and a couple of families from a neighbouring village called Premier. Not so long, as he said.

Séraphin went back to stoking the fire, on which he had thrown a couple of branches of pine. The branches flared up so that you could see both men clearly, sitting face-to-face, either side of the hearth, each on the end of his bench: one already old, dried up, tallish, with small, pale eyes embedded in browless orbits under an old felt hat; the other much younger, between twenty and twenty-five, with a white shirt, a brown jacket, a little black moustache and black hair trimmed short.

"As if you were at the other end of the world," said Séraphin, "As if you were never going to see her again…"

He nodded, stopped talking.

Antoine had only been married two months, and it should be stated at the outset that this marriage had not come about without some difficulty. As an orphan he had been sent into service at the age of thirteen, to work for a family in the village, while his beloved came from money. For a long time her mother wouldn't hear of a son-in-law who couldn't bring his fair share to the household. For a long time old Philomène shook her head, saying, "No!", then, "No!" and "No!" again. Who knows what would have happened if Séraphin hadn't been there, exactly where he was needed, that is, and could make a difference? As the brother of Philomène, the widow Maye, and unmarried himself, it was from him that his sister took her lead. Well Séraphin had taken Antoine's side, and in the end he had got his way.

The wedding had taken place in April. Now Séraphin and Antoine were, as we say, *en montagne.*

It's the custom of the people of Aïre, around the fifteenth of June, to lead their herds up to the high pastures, including the one at Derborence where these two found themselves that evening, Séraphin having taken Antoine along to show him the ropes, since he was beginning to feel his age. He limped, he had a stiff leg. With the rheumatism that had recently set in in his left shoulder, so that it too had become less obliging, life had become difficult in all sorts of ways. The work in the mountain chalets waits for no man, the cows have to be milked twice a day, butter or cheese has to be made every day. So Séraphin had taken Antoine with him in the hope that Antoine would soon be in a position to take over. In the event, Antoine hadn't leapt at the challenge. He was pining for his wife.

"Come," he tried again, "it could be worse. Is it really so terrible to have me along for company?"

He was only thinking of Antoine.

It was to Antoine that he had spoken, in front of the fire, that evening of the twenty-second of June, around nine. And as the flames began to die down again he fed them, reviving them with a few more branches of pine.

"Never!" said Antoine.

That was all, he shut up again. And Séraphin shut up too, at that moment, both of them having become aware of something inhuman expanding around them, something that couldn't be endured for long: silence. The silence of the high mountains, the silence of those human deserts where man appears only fleetingly. You cock an ear on the offchance that it's you in fact who is silent, but you hear only that you hear nothing. It was as if nothing existed anywhere, from here to the end of the world, from here to the bottom of the sky. Nothing, emptiness, the void, the perfection of the void; a total ceasing to be, as if the world had yet to be created, or was no longer, as if you were here before its beginning or long after its end. And anxiety gathers in your chest as if a hand were squeezing your heart.

Luckily the fire begins to sizzle again, or a drop of water falls, or a breath of wind grazes the roof. The slightest little sound is deafening. The drop falls resoundingly. The branch gnawed by the flame cracks like a gunshot. The wind's teasing alone fills the vastness of that space. All kinds of tiny noises, grown immense, rebound. You come to life again because they are alive.

"See here," said Séraphin.

The fire crackled again.

"If you want to go down on Saturday… You could always stay a couple of days in the village, spend Sunday with her."

"What about you?"

"Oh don't worry about me, I'm used to my own company."

He smiled into his beard that was almost white, though his moustache was still black – it was about nine in the evening, on the twenty-second of June, in Derborence, in the chalet that belonged to Philomène, where the two men sat in front of the fire.

Something snapped now and then in the roof.

Séraphin went on: "Come back when you want. I'll manage, I always do. And if you do come back, you won't be alone here."

He smiled into his white beard, fixing Antoine with his little grey eyes: "Unless I don't count?"

"Oh!" said Antoine.

Something gave again in the roof which, made of beams and large flat stones, rose obliquely above them to a point, the chalet having been built against a rocky outcrop.

"It's agreed then, for Saturday. Only three days to wait."

The roof cracked. The blocks of slate, exposed to the sun in the daytime, expand in its heat. But with the cool of evening they shrink again, making sudden, widely spaced noises, as if someone were walking about up there. As if a burglar had put his foot down carefully, then stopped to listen, making sure nobody had heard him before taking another step. It cracked, then it stopped cracking, and under the roof that had once again fallen silent, they saw each other, then they didn't. The flame surges, the flame dies back.

But Antoine had lifted his head: a new kind of sound had made itself heard. Not the noises in the roof any more, but something less audible, something from the depths of space. The rumble of thunder, perhaps, preceded by a muffled detonation. And though it carried on, it was now interspersed with shocks that were themselves prolonged by their own echoes.

"Ah!" said Séraphin. "They're starting again."

"Who?"

"You mean you didn't hear them, these last nights? Good for you, you must sleep deeply. And you don't know these parts yet. Up there, see… Remember the name of the mountain…? Yes, the ridge with the glacier… The Devils' Place."

The noise faded, became faint, almost imperceptible, as when a current of air stirs the leaves on the trees.

"You know what they say, don't you? That he lives up there, on the glacier, with his wife and children."

The noise had faded to nothing.

"And that sometimes, when he's bored, he says to his devil's spawn, 'Get the pucks.' That's the skittle up there, the devil's skittle. And they play a game. They try to hit the skittle with their pucks. Beautiful pucks, I tell you, made from precious stones: blue, green, transparent… But every now and then they miss the target and guess where they end up, those missiles. What comes after the edge of the glacier, eh? Nothing, the void. The pucks fall, you see them sometimes, if the moon's up, as it is now…"

He said, "Want to come and see?"

Was Antoine afraid? Who knows, but he was curious, and since Séraphin got up, so did he. Séraphin went first, he opened the door. You saw the moon was indeed up, its light fell in bright, brilliant blocks onto the clay floor behind them.

There was a grassy space, a flat space with some chalets on it. A sort of prairie, but narrowly enclosed by the rocks that towered above it on all sides. Looking first to the south, to the cluster of peaks at whose feet they stood, the two men saw where the moon had risen. Then, turning to where it would set, they saw where the walls of rock began, where those ramparts were still not very high, before they continued in a half-circle to the north and east.

Séraphin raised his arm. You saw his hand in the bright night, you saw that his index finger was extended; that it was almost directly over his head. You were obliged to tilt your own head back to the same degree. Séraphin was pointing to something high up, fifteen hundred metres above you.

You saw clearly now that on that side too, on the north side, that is, you were com-

4

pletely enclosed, and on the side where the moon rose too, where there's an opening that's hidden by the mountain in the foreground. Séraphin raises his arm, he conjures up before us a new wall, higher than the others, and we understand that we are at the bottom of a crater. We see, nevertheless, how that great palisade is riddled from top to bottom with narrow gorges in which small waterfalls hang, shivering. Our gaze runs up it, until Séraphin's finger brings it to a halt.

He was pointing to something at the top, something on the ridge itself. Where the ridge jutted out, and a thick layer of glacier covered it up to the brink of the void. A faint light emanated from there: a luminous fringe, vaguely transparent, with tints of green and blue and a phosphorescent glow. It was the fault in the ice up there, also, at this hour, full of silence and peace. Nothing moved anywhere under the intangible dust of the moonlight; the dust you saw floating lazily in the air or settling in a thin layer over things, wherever it found a surface to cling to.

"Up there…"

Séraphin's arm was still raised. He said, "Yes, there, where it sticks out. But it looks as if it's all over for this evening."

His voice boomed in the silence.

"Oh!" he went on. "It's always been that way, for as long as anyone can remember."

He had lowered his arm.

"The ancients talked about it in their day. And when they were little they heard their ancients talking about it. It's unpredictable, is all. Pity…"

From time to time you heard a bell tinkling around a goat's neck, somewhere close by. The chalets, dry stone cabins, were scattered all about. One side of each roof was lit by the moon, as if it were blanketed with snow. The other merged with the shadow it threw onto the ground.

The two men waited a moment longer in case something happened, but nothing did.

From time to time, at most, a breath of wind carried to your ear the distant whisper of a waterfall. The breath itself ran close to the ground, like when your hand brushes over the nap of some soft stuff. Beasts and men slumbered. Up there, on the other hand…

Up there, where they are still looking, there is only that thin fringe of ice in the moonlight, so fine, so wisplike that you sometimes seem to see it stir like a thread lifted on the breeze. Antoine thought he saw it stir, he was about to say so to Séraphin, but the latter was shaking his head: "I think the devil has gone to bed; maybe we should do the same?"

So Antoine said nothing, and the two of them went back into the chalet, closing the door behind them.

They stretched out on straw mattresses laid on planks that had been fixed to the wall to form two bunks. They slept one above the other, as on a boat.

Antoine slept in the top bunk.

They hung their boots from a hook by their laces, because of the rats.

Antoine climbed up to his bunk.

"Good night," Séraphin said.

"Good night," he replied.

And right away there she was, in his dreams, as soon as he rolled himself up in his brown wool blanket and turned to the wall. Thérèse. But what's wrong?

She was back, her and the fields, having found room for themselves in the narrow space between Antoine and the wall. He said hello, she said hello. He said, "So?", she said, "So." They had to arrange to meet far from the village, away from prying eyes. There are always spies, always people interfering in things that don't concern them. She had a rake over her shoulder. He noticed how, with the teeth of her rake, she hooked the clouds as she went by. The clouds fell on her head. Why had he sat higher than her on the slope? He could only see her from behind and she was leaning forward, revealing a strip of brown skin between her bun and her red scarf.

"Is something the matter?"

"Oh, not with me," she said.

"Who then?"

"My mother."

That was when things weren't going well.

She began to slide. He said, "Wait for me!" She slid faster and faster on her behind, though she herself made not the slightest movement. The ground seemed simply to fall away from her. She sped faster and faster, but he sped too, so that the distance between them stayed the same, so that he could still speak to her and she could reply. They flew along. "Watch out for the Rhone!" he said. Because at the bottom was the

Rhone and, he thought, it's not winter. "Mother says that if we have children we'll have nothing to live on."

Look out!

There was a crash. Was he still asleep?

The strange noise that he thought he'd heard was still there.

Is it in his head? In his ears is the sound of water. He's sleeping, or is he? He turns, sees the door of the chalet open. Someone pushes their head carefully into the moonlight which stops halfway down their back, falling in a straight line.

Where is she?

"Ah!" he says. "Everything's been straightened out since then. Sure it has. We're married now, it's done. That was before."

He thinks, "Saturday…"

He opens his eyes again. He sees that whoever it was has left. The square of moonlight behind the door is as empty as a blank canvas.

He went back to sleep. Or did he?

Then the roof caved in, and one of the beams supporting it crashed into the wooden shelf where Antoine lay on his mattress.

II

Derborence: the word sings softly, softly and a little sadly in your head. It starts out quite strongly, with determination, then falters and fades until, by the end, it has emptied itself out, as if signifying ruin, abandon, oblivion.

The place it names is desolate now. No herd goes up there, man himself has turned his back on it. It's five or six hours from the plain if you're coming from the west, that is from the Vaud. Where is it, this Derborence? "It's back there," they'll tell you. You have to climb a long way against the current of a stream whose water is so clear it flows like air over its bed of stones. Derborence, to get there you must slowly haul yourself up two long, uneven ridges; ridges like knives whose backs are sunk in the earth while the nicked steel of their blades shines in places and in others is eaten away by rust. To left and right they rise ever higher, these ridges, climbing as you climb, and the word continues to chant softly in your head as you pass close to the fine chalets of those lower slopes. Long chalets, that have been properly rendered and whitewashed, with roofs made of wooden tiles like fish scales. Chalets that have byres for the beasts and fountains that overflow.

You continue to climb, the slope gets steeper. By now you've reached the wide pastures that are cleaved into storeys by stony outgrowths. You pass from one storey to the next. You're not far from Derborence now, not far from the land of glaciers either, because the long ascent brings you eventually to a pass that was formed by the concertinaing of the mountain chains above the pastures and chalets of Anzeindaz. Anzeindaz, where the chalets form a little village high above the treeline, just before the grass runs out.

Derborence is close now. Just keep going.

Suddenly, there's no more ground beneath your feet.

Suddenly the line of pasture, rubbing itself out in the middle, starts to trace a hollow curve out of nothing at all. You know you've arrived because an immense hole opens up in front of you. A hole in the form of an oval, like a huge basket with sheer sides. You have to lean over to see into it, because you're at nearly two thousand metres and the bottom is five or six hundred metres below you.

You lean over, you stick your neck out. You feel cold air on your face.

Derborence is first of all a taste of winter at the height of summer, because it lies in shade almost all day long, even when the sun is at its zenith. And you see that all there is down there is stone, stone and more stone.

Above you, too, the walls plunge sheer on every side, higher or less high, smoother or less smooth, while the path slithers downwards, twisting and turning like a worm. And wherever you look, in front of you, to your left, to your right, there is, upright or prone, suspended in the air or fallen down, there is, rearing up in spurs or shrinking back, or even folding itself into narrow gorges, rock, nothing but rock, everywhere the same desolate rock.

The sun, where it reaches, colours the rock in myriad ways, because one series of peaks throws its shadow onto the other, the one to the south on the one to the north. And you see that the ridge is the yellow of ripe grapes in one place, and pink as a rose in another.

But the shadow is already climbing, climbing. It inches irresistibly higher, like the water in the bowl of a fountain, and as it climbs, all is extinguished, all cools, all is silenced, shrivels and dies. Meanwhile one melancholy hue, a bluish tint, spreads like a fine fog beneath you, and through it you spy two small, sad lakes that gleam for a little longer, then gleam no more, lying flat among the disorder like a pair of zinc roofs.

Because there is still that bottom, but look closely: nothing moves there. Look long and hard: all is stillness. Look: from the towering cliffs in the north to those in the south, there's nowhere for life to get a foothold. On the contrary, all is buried beneath its antithesis.

Something has filled that space between what is alive and us. It begins as sand in the form of a cone whose point is half buried in the wall to the north. From there it spills out, like dice from a cup, just like dice in fact, dice of all sizes, one square block, another square block, blocks on blocks, blocks after blocks, large and small, covering up those depths until they're lost to view.

And yet in the old days they went up to Derborence in large numbers. Close to fifty, they say, some years. They reached it by the gorge that, at its other end, empties into the Rhone. They came from Aïre and Premier, valaisan villages perched high on the northern side of the Rhone valley.

They decamped around the middle of June, with their little brown cows and their goats, moving into the chalets they had built themselves up there out of dry stone and sheets of slate, and they stayed two or three months.

From May on, in those days, the bottom was painted a beautiful shade of green, since up there it's the month of May that wields the paintbrush.

Up there (those from the Valais say "up there", while those from Anzeindaz say "down there" or "at the bottom"), when the snow retreats, it leaves behind large drifts. At the edge of these, in the black dampness covered by patches of old grass as by a sort of drab felt, they would discover every kind of little flower pushing up around a layer of ice thinner than a pane of glass. Mountain flowers with their extraordinary radiance, their extraordinary purity, their extraordinary colours: whiter than snow, bluer than the sky, vivid orange or violet: croci, anemones, the primroses so coveted by pharmacists. Seen from afar, they form bright splashes amid the shrinking grey stains left by the snow. Like the pattern on a silk scarf, one of those scarves the girls buy in town when they go down to the fair of Saint Peter or Saint Joseph. Then it's the colour of the material itself that changes, no more grey and white but an explosion of green everywhere. It's the sap rising, it's the grass showing its head again, as if the artist had scattered green drops from his brush, and they had bled into one another.

Ah Derborence! You were beautiful then, beautiful and pleasant and welcoming, readying yourself from the first days of June for the men who would come. They waited only for that sign from you. Then one afternoon, the dull roar of the torrent in the gorge would be punctured and split and another sound would pierce it: the clanging of a cowbell. You saw the first cow appear, then ten, then fifteen, then as many as a hundred.

The little goatherd blew his horn.

They lit fires in the chalets. Above every chimneytop or doorcrack, a pretty wisp of blue hung in the still air.

The smoke grew, flattened out. Higher up it formed a sort of translucent ceiling, like a spider's web stretched between the rock walls high above you.

Beneath that web, life found its rhythm again and carried on, with those roofs dotted about, not far apart, like little books on a green carpet, all those roofs bound in grey; with two or three little streams, flashing like a raised sword; with round dots and oval dots moving about all over, the round dots being men and the oval ones cows.

When Derborence was still inhabited, before the mountain fell down.

Now, though, it has just fallen down.

III

The ones from Anzeindaz said, "It started with a burst of artillery, all six big guns going off at once."

"Then," they said, "a strong gust blew through."

"Then there was gunfire, explosions, loud bangs, detonations on all sides, as if someone were shooting at us, as if the whole mountain had opened fire."

"The wind kneed the door wide open. The ash from the hearth started falling on our heads as if it were snowing in the chalet..."

"Here on the pass, see, we're not far beneath the place where the slide started, though a little behind it and to one side, and the first noise we heard was the splitting of the overhang when it came away. After that it was as if the mountains had declared war on one another. Thunder seemed to reverberate around each peak in that semi-circle, moving from one to the next, from the Argentine to the Dents-de-Morcles, from the Rochers-du-Vent to Saint-Martin."

They were already on their feet. There were three of them. They couldn't find their torch.

The cows had been brought in for the night, but not tied up, and they were making a terrible racket in the byre, threatening to bring everything crashing down. The men had to go and calm them.

They had a lantern with glass panes that they wouldn't otherwise have needed, the night being moonlit. Soon, though, they were astonished to see the moon darken and dim, as when there is an eclipse, while the light of the lamp grew stronger, casting a bright disk onto the grass at their feet.

And it was thanks to the lamp that they saw that great pale cloud rise up before them. Little by little silence returned, but the cloud grew and grew behind the ridge that still obscured the depths of Derborence from their view, as if a wall were rising out of a wall. It was like a huge cloud of smoke, but flat, not billowing; slower and heavier than fog; top-heavy, like dough rising, like when the baker places the dough in a tin and it expands and spills over the rim.

It was the mountain that had fallen down.

The men coughed, they sneezed, they lowered their heads, trying to protect themselves behind the brims of their hats.

But it was a fine powder, an impalpable dust that, hanging in the air, penetrated everything, and they had no choice but to thrust themselves into it, because by now it was on top of them. They took a few steps inside it, then a few more, then stopped. One of them even said, "Is it safe to go on?"

The same one said, "Is it solid underfoot? If we can't see…"

They pushed on anyway, out of pride, out of curiosity.

Besides, the noises were becoming fewer and further between, more and more inaudible, retreating inside, as if something were slowly being digested. Now they came from beneath you, from deep in the earth, such that the three men could advance easily to the edge of the hole, to the pass.

They saw nothing. They saw only that churning white mass. One moment they were blind, another a chink or a tear opened up in the cloud. These they saw, but nothing else. They hid not only the bottom of the crater, but also the walls around it, so you could see neither where the rockslide had begun, nor the slide itself. All you could make out was that mass of vapour, as if you were peering into a washtub. All you could make out was confusion, lit vaguely by the moon, reddened by it, because the moon was red in the sky, then it disappeared, then it reappeared.

The lantern which stood beside the men dimmed, rallied, dimmed again. They lay on their bellies, only venturing the tops of their heads over that rim, only the forehead and the eyes.

One said, "How many, do you think?"

"Good god!"

The third one said, "Depends if they had all come up already… Fifteen, twenty?"

Coughing still, but used by now to the lack of air, they stayed where they were, talking in low voices. From time to time there was a groaning beneath them, and because they lay with their stomachs pressed to the mountain, they heard it through their stomachs. The noises reverberated the length of their bodies to reach their ears.

The men from Sanetsch ran too, the ones from the northwest, that is, from the other side of that great wall. They stopped above the Woodcarrier's Passage, which plunges precipitously to the bottom via flues in the rock. They spoke to each other in their language, a language we don't understand because it's a remnant of German. They spoke and at the same time they made gestures nobody could see, not even themselves. To get there they had had to cross a karst plateau, which is to say a rocky waste that has been sculpted over eons by rainwater and resembles a frozen sea, complete with crests, folds and overhangs, and riddled with sinkholes (places where the water had see-sawed). And they too interrogated the depths from which rose, like a reply, inexplicable grumblings, growlings devoid of meaning; out of which came only strange tongues and vortices of dust.

They were caught up in it, in their mouths they tasted crushed slate. They were swallowed by one wave, then by another; enveloped, released, enveloped again.

As for the ones from Zamperon, they clung to their mattresses until daybreak. Zamperon, which consists of three or four chalets, is the destination of the people of Premier, the neighbouring village to Aïre. Three or four chalets a little lower down than Derborence, between Derborence and the gorge that tumbles to the Rhone. Its inhabitants found themselves in the path of the wind that rushed through, that ripped the stones off roofs, even lifting the entire roof off two or three of the little hay-lofts there, tossing them long distances as if they were straw hats. It scythed through a stand of young trees that grew on an outcrop of mountain and insinuated itself through cracks in uncemented walls to reach the men laid out on their mattresses, prodding them as if with the point of a stick and pushing them to the bottoms of their bunks.

You heard the tubs of cheeses come tumbling down, you heard the benches crash to the floor. The doors rattled as if someone were shaking them with both hands. The world shifted and groaned, splintered and whistled. It all happened at once; in the air, on the ground and under the earth. In that confusion of elements you could no longer distinguish sound from movement, nor what the sounds meant, nor where they came from, nor where they were going, as if the world were ending. Gripping their bedframes to avoid being tossed to the ground, the inhabitants of Zamperon flattened themselves rigid, more dead than alive. Paralysed, speechless, mouths agape in terror, mouths filled with silence, shaken, their limbs lifeless, they had long ago stopped moving. Then little by little, calm returned. Little by little the noise died and you heard nothing but muted shiftings, distant slidings. Still they didn't speak, still they didn't call out to one another.

Not until first light which, happily, comes early at this time of year. By half past three, as a rule, something pale and uncertain is shimmering over the eastern ridges, knocking the stars out of the sky one by one like so many ripe fruit. That day, there was no mountain, there were no ridges and no sun either. The sluggish day announced itself reluctantly and late, and instead of making an appearance at one point in the sky, it was somehow everywhere at once. A yellow fog entirely filled the space, and this astonished the first man to emerge from his chalet, as it astonished

13

him to find himself inside it, and something else astonished him too, though he didn't yet know what it was.

His name was Biollaz. He was from Premier.

Having sat up on his mattress, because by now you could just about see, he called out to his comrade, "Are you coming?" No reply. He called again, "Loutre! Hey, Loutre!" Still no reply. "Or are you dead?"

He glimpsed the sky through a hole that the previous night's wind had torn in the roof. The hole was directly above him, it was big enough for a man to pass through. And since no-one answered him, he pulled one leg out from beneath the cover, a trousered leg since he slept in his clothes, and paused to listen. Still nothing, so he pulled out the other leg. "Loutre?"

Loutre had moved at last.

Biollaz saw Loutre watching him from where he lay on his own bed. "Are you coming?" The other shook his head. "Suit yourself, I'm going anyway."

Biollaz stands up. Daylight now fills the room, thanks to the hole in the roof, so that he moves easily through it, observing that in the chalet everything is now on the floor, that the things that had been hung from hooks or placed on shelves had left their hooks and shelves, that the pails of milk had been overturned.

Having put on his shoes, Biollaz picks his way between the puddles to the door.

He tries to open it; the door no longer opens. A part of the wall has caved in, warping the doorframe.

He has to climb out through the hole in the roof.

Loutre gives him a leg up and supports him from underneath. Having reached the opening he leans back in, holding out his hands to Loutre. Being the first to jump down from the roof, he marvels at the fog that envelops him, marvels at the silence pressing in on all sides.

Something is missing, something that was is no more: the sound of the torrent no longer reaches his ears, though at this time of year it is usually at its fullest.

"Loutre, Loutre, where are you?"

Loutre: "Here."

"Loutre, do you hear? The Lizerne…"

Loutre: "I'm coming."

They're together outside. They move along the path littered with slates that the wind had transported there, and that had smashed on landing revealing fibres as in wood.

Others come out of their houses.

They can only just make each other out in the distance, and when they come closer they still don't recognise one another. They frighten themselves, their faces are so changed. They barely speak. They sigh, they look at one another, they shake their heads. They come to the Donneloye house. The door opens. A boy emerges, looks at them. Has he seen them? Taking off, he runs along the path that leads down to the valley. They call after him, "Hey, Dsozet!" He doesn't hear. They call him but he has disappeared already, swallowed up by the opaque air that lifts and falls back behind him like a heavy curtain.

They carry on along the path that leads to Derborence. It's no more than a quarter of an hour by foot. They struggle through a fog that's like layers of dirty wadding, arranged one in front of the other with pockets of air between them; like the pages of a book bound at a spine somewhere above them, that fan open below. The layers were becoming frayed, allowing more and more light through. Finally they could see. Having stopped on the path, they saw that it was blocked. There was a sort of barricade across it, like a fortress rising up before them with ramparts, parapets, slits for archers. This barricade had come down in the night, but from where? They couldn't yet see. But there it was, in front of them, a barrage of blocks large and small, of sand, gravel and mortar, and meanwhile the bed of the torrent that emerged from it was dry, except for the odd puddle.

"Halt!"

"Who's that?"

It was old Plan who watches the sheep in the high ravines of the Derbonère.

To their left, to the southwest, a corridor opened up high in the mountain, a steep corridor so rocky and arid that only sheep used it.

They saw the flock come rattling down it like a cascade of pebbles.

They saw it huddle in a hollow, like a small loch whose surface a passing gust has turned choppy.

They saw it stray over the slopes like the shadow of a cloud.

They saw it, and in front of it was old Plan.

"Halt!"

Perched on a high rock, he held up his hand.

"Go no further!"

He nodded into his white beard, he wore a long greatcoat. It was the colour of rust, the colour of moss, the colour of bark, the colour of stone. It was the colour of things in nature, having long been exposed, like them, to radiant suns, showers, snow, cold, heat, wind, violent transformations, balmy airs, the long succession of days and nights.

"Go no further! D... E..."

He laughed.

"D... E... V... Get it?"

As he was speaking, something moved up there, among the rocks. Someone was coming through, or trying to.

They see that it's a man, but having taken a step he can barely hold himself upright. Steadying himself by placing both hands on the nearest rock, he tries to take another step and keels over on his side.

They look, then they look harder.

"It's Barthelémy!" they cry.

And as they run towards him, they hear old Plan shouting.

"Danger! No further... Stop! Stop!"

IV

The evening before, Thérèse sat down on the bench in front of their house. She wore a dress, brown with many pleats, from which emerged the sleeves of her rough hemp blouse. She was slumped forward, with her elbows on her knees, her gaze angled downwards, over the tops of the trees in the orchard, down the slope, down, down to the bottom of the valley, to the plain, that vast plain smooth as paper through which flows the Rhone.

How time drags! Eight days since Antoine left and it feels like eight months!

Letting her head droop, she saw the Rhone against a flat green backcloth. It was grey and white, its bed being too wide for it because of all the sand and stones it had brought down and deposited at its edges (that's why they've channelled it since).

It was scored there like a road on a map, the bed that is, twisting and turning with its lemon-grey borders. The river itself ran between them, and you saw it moving in the middle, being of a lighter grey, almost white, sliding on its belly like an adder.

That's always there too, it never changes. Oh I know the Rhone alright, I know it only too well!

It tells its age-old tale, she thought, the same one over and over since the beginning of time (you'd hear it if you listened carefully, you hear it better at night).

Maybe Antoine will come on Sunday, but he'll have to go back up again. No sooner have we found each other than we're separated. No sooner married than unmarried; brought together, split apart. If only Antoine could come back for good! Here I am staring at the Rhone, and I never give it a second thought when we're together!

I'm bored, so bored!

You could hear people walking past the house on the other side, going home to eat their soup.

The day was over. It started at four in the morning, it finished at eight at night.

They were heading home. You could hear the sound of their footsteps, sometimes muted, sometimes creaking, muted by the mud or creaking because of the large flat stones that had been placed over it here and there, as over a ford.

On this side of the village the façades of the houses are two-tone, white below and brown above; on the other, the back of the house, which is lower, overlooks a narrow alley that runs between the houses and another row of buildings. From the front, then, these houses appear black and white, neat as beehives in a garden; from the back they're black and higgledy-piggledy, and they cast a shadow over the permanently muddy alleyway. There was no-one to be seen in front of these houses, but behind them, people came and went, women with rakes over their shoulders, little girls carrying buckets of water, and the odd man, because this is the village in summer, and almost all the young and fit have left for the mountains, leaving behind only the sick and the old, the poor and the stupid.

It was a beautiful day. Between her feet she watched some little red ants carry their eggs in single file along a groove they had worn in the dust – a kind of alley itself, she thought, because ants are like us, ants with their eggs that are bigger than them, us with our outsized bundles of hay...

She felt hot all over, the blood roared in her ears. She had trouble breathing even though she had sat up straight. She was flushed, she turned pale, she flushed again.

What's happening?

She ponders, and an idea comes to her: after all she's married, she's been married two months.

Could it really be that?

She changes colour again. That must be it, she says to herself. If not that, then what? She's healthy enough.

It has to be that. She changes colour again, smiles. Having put her head between her knees, she leans back against the wall, cushioning her head against her bun, and her lips are once more as red as her scarf.

Feeling better, she stays put. "If it's that... if it is that, I'll never be alone again. There'll be two of us when he's away, and three of us when he comes back."

Opposite her, on a level with her eyes, are the mountains. Not one, not two, not ten, but hundreds of them, laid out in a half-moon like a garland of flowers hovering at the bottom of the sky.

There above the forests, above the pastures, above the rock, there where the snows and the many-coloured ice float as if detached from that which holds them up, from the foundations that the day has already thrown into shadow.

The more the shadow deepens beneath them, the lighter and more luminous they appear, revealing their pinks and reds, their shades of gold and silver.

It gladdens her heart. In April, when they were married, the peach trees were in bloom. This is a promise that they will bloom again. Her eye wanders back over the range: it really is like when the peach blossoms, when the wild rosebuds open, when the quince, more hesitant, more timid, slower than the others, at last puts on its display; because the mountains have just now begun to pale. They fade, turn grey, but what does it matter, she thinks, because tomorrow they will flower again.

The alley was deserted. The women called their children. They came to the threshold, called a name several times, called it again. Thérèse realised she had lost track of time. Her mother would be waiting for her, because since Antoine had gone she had been eating her meals at her mother's house.

She ran. She cut across the gardens so as not to bump into anyone and have to stop and waste even more time. She saw the red square of the door at the top of the steps and climbed up to it, clutching the rail since she felt lightheaded.

"Not before time!" a voice called. "Where have you been?"

You saw Philomène all in black in front of the stove over which the pot hung. She turned towards Thérèse as she entered and said, "Hurry up, light the lamps."

Thérèse takes a larch twig – this evening of the twenty-second of June, around half past eight, as Séraphin and Antoine sit in front of the fire in Derborence. They are in front of the fire, Séraphin and Antoine, the stars are appearing one by one, the moon has yet to rise. In the big dark kitchen there is one point of light, the fire, and her mother is in front of it. Thérèse takes the twig and with her twig she approaches the fire – the twenty-second of June. She comes away, holding between her hands, which are lit up on the inside, the tiny, trembling flame, she brings it close to the oily wick of the lamp that hangs by a chain from a beam.

On the table of polished walnut two tin plates had been laid opposite one another.

Philomène brings the pot and places it on a pine disk made for that purpose, then sits down without another word.

Philomène eats her soup. It's the twenty-second of June, and meanwhile, six hundred metres below, at the bottom of the valley, the Rhone crawls on its belly, sweeping over the stones and leaving a light rustling sound on the air, as when someone walks through dry leaves. Suddenly Philomène stops eating, her big tin spoon halfway to her mouth, and glances at her daughter.

"What is it?"

"Nothing."

"So why aren't you eating?"

"I don't know," said Thérèse. "I'm not hungry."

Philomène shrugged.

"Oh I see, it's because he's not here. Poor child, you're not the first, you know… I was married once too… And it was the same for me, when your poor papa went to the mountains, he left me alone all summer…"

She spoke harshly, unaware that the old bitterness had left its trace in her voice. She went on: "Anyway, you chose him, that husband of yours. You were born here, you know the custom. You know we're widows for at least two months of the year."

Thérèse shook her head.

"It's not that."

"Then what?"

"I don't know…"

The twenty-second of June around nine in the evening, beneath the oil lamp with its tiny flame in the shape of an upside-down heart.

"You don't know?"

"I feel sick…"

"Sick?"

"Yes, and dizzy."

"Ah!" said Philomène. "Since when?"

"Since today."

"Is it your time of the month?"

"Yes."

Thérèse fell quiet. And you saw Philomène smile as she looked at her, something she hadn't done since her daughter's wedding day. Then: "That's a good illness," she said. "It's one of those illnesses you give thanks for, when they come to call."

Meanwhile Thérèse felt the blood rush to her cheeks, like a warm tide surging beneath her skin. Then it retreated again.

"It must be that," said Philomène. "Oh, it's a good illness, that one! You mustn't be afraid, and you mustn't force yourself. If you don't feel hungry, don't eat… I'll make you a cup of camomile and you can go to bed…"

She said, "He doesn't know, of course? Oh, he has a lovely surprise in store for him!"

Thérèse had gone to bed. That was in their house, a house that had been done up especially for them. The bed was big and made of larch, a square bed, as long as it was wide, and which, fixed to the wall by hooks, reached almost to the ceiling on its tall legs.

I can sprawl across it when he's not here.

But he'll be back soon, he'll come back down from the mountain. And when he does, I'll tell him, "Your bed awaits you, my lord."

She amused herself by talking to him as if he were there beside her. She'd say, "You smell of the mountains, you smell of woodsmoke and goat… No matter, my lord, lie close to me anyway, because I'm cold and lonely."

Why did they make us such a big bed, if not for us to be together in it?

"I can lie lengthways, you see, but I can also lie crossways if I like. Oh I'm bored, come quickly!"

She'd tell him, "Lie there, but no touching… First I have something to tell you. It's a secret… Promise you won't tell anyone… Promise?"

I'll hold his hands if necessary. I'll tell him, "No touching… Oh my lord, my handsome lord, that's not allowed!"

And he'd say, "A little kiss, just one…"

She would say, "Where?" "On the white of the eye." "No, first I have to tell you something. Turn your face to the ceiling, I'll lay my head sideways, that way your beard won't scratch me and my mouth will be close to your ear, all the better to tell you the secret, Antoine…"

She turned over again in the big bed and the hours of the night began to file past. She might have dozed off.

It must have been stormy.

He said, "This secret, what is it? Money? A visit?"

She said, "Guess!"

The storm blows. The noise, which began in her dream, slips into reality. She opens her eyes, it's still there. It's thunder, rumbling over the mountains to the north. She hears it coming closer, punctuated by violent jolts, like a cart loaded with pine trunks that roll into one another. It passes overhead. Finally it runs into the southern side of the valley, bouncing off it.

Travelling backwards, it collides with itself.

The shutters rattle, a ladder falls. The windows in Thérèse's bedroom, which hadn't been properly closed, blow wide open.

She feels cold in her shift as she runs to close them, and at the same time she sees that there is no lightning, even though the thunder continues to swirl and boom over the roof.

She sees that it's a beautiful night and that the trees, bathed in moonlight, have contorted themselves into strange shapes, raising their branches on which the leaves stand upright like the hairs on your arm. Falling again, they become still and the leaves regain their usual roundness beneath that soft, bright rain that streams over their surface as over sleek feathers.

What's going on?

She hears voices in the street, there's a window in the kitchen that gives onto that side. She hurries to the kitchen, she is naked beneath her shift, and barefoot. The thunder recedes.

There were a few more cracking sounds, noises like the wooden frame of a bedroom makes when the temperature changes. Then everything seemed to become peaceful again, except that now windows and doors were opening in the village. Heads appeared at windows, people emerged from their doors, saying, "What is it?"

They turn to each other, they look up. They see that the stars are in their usual places: one big red one, one green, one small and white, between the roofs. Pointed ones, round ones, ones that move, others that don't. They say, "That was no storm."

She didn't dare show herself.

The men had pulled on trousers, the women had put skirts on over their shifts. A woman's voice calls, "Hey, anyone know what that was?"

She doesn't dare show herself, her shift doesn't fit properly, it slips off her shoulders.

"Do we ever know? The mountain cuts the world in two. One day it's fine here, but filthy where the Germans are."

They looked toward the mountain which was visible in places, to the north, between the houses. All was calm, right up to the ridge.

"You think? We would have seen the glow."

"What glow?"

"Lightning…"

"They could be blasting the mines," one said.

"You're off your head. I say an earthquake. My bed moved under me."

"Mine too."

"No, it's a barrel I stashed badly," said one of the Carrupts, because they're almost all Carrupts in Aïre. "It must have rolled down to the cellar door."

The men were black and white in the moonlight. The women were black stains blotting the lighted windows from which they leaned.

"But the noise?"

"Oh!" said another. "Earthquakes make a lot of noise."

"And the wind?"

"The wind goes with it."

"You think?"

"I know."

"What now then?"

"It's all over."

"We go back to bed?"

"What time is it?" someone asked.

"Half past two."

It is now the twenty-third of June.

Thérèse stays to listen but the doors close one by one, the windows too. Everything is peaceful on earth as in the sky and in the village around her, where the only sound is the babbling of a fountain that has made itself heard again and won't stop, now, until morning.

V

Only Maurice Nendaz guessed what had happened; a lame man who walked with a cane.

He had once broken his thigh cutting wood in the forest, the left thigh. It had set badly, so that now it formed an angle with itself, and the left leg was shorter than the right.

With each step, he stumbled sideways.

He advanced a little further along the alley, as the windows shut and the sound of closing doors faded away. Then, from behind the corner of a shed, he called softly, "Hey, Justin!"

Justin was one of his neighbours, a young man of fifteen or sixteen who had not yet gone in.

"Are you sleepy?" Nendaz asked him. "No? In that case, get your coat and come with me."

"Where are you going?"

"You'll see."

Justin went to fetch a jacket. As for Nendaz, he was ready to leave, hat on head, stick in hand.

"You didn't breathe a word? Good! Let them sleep in peace for a little while longer."

You heard the sound he made with his stick on the stones; you heard the sound his bad leg made, because it struck the ground harder than the other when he shifted his weight to it.

As soon as you leave the village, the path that leads to Derborence begins to climb, traversing the hillside where rock ledges rise out of one another, and nothing grows between them but a few thorny bushes and some stunted pines with red trunks. In daylight, you can clearly see the oblique it traces; it's as straight as if it had been drawn with a ruler. You follow it with your eye until, suddenly, it vanishes into an opening in the rock two hundred metres higher up. At that hour, however, and because the moon had just hidden itself, they could barely make out the ground, which was very uneven, and since they had no lamp they made slow progress. Pebbles shifted under the soles of their boots, the shale slithered over itself, and they stubbed their toes against protruding stones. They proceeded cautiously, therefore, and Nendaz took the lead, since he also had to rein in his bad leg, which wasn't easy. He didn't speak. You saw him totter sideways, right himself, then totter again, pressing down with his right hand on the head of his cane. You heard him breathing hard with the effort. From time to time, he paused without turning round. Then Justin paused too, brought up short by the shadow that loomed in front of him, that was darker than the rest; a headless shadow, since Nendaz was bent forward. By now a dash of white had blended itself with the air, as when you let a drop of some light colour fall into a pot of a darker one, stirring it all the time.

They were approaching the end of the straight line that the path made against the slope, after which it ran out. The black all around them began to give way to grey, and the grey became lighter and more transparent until things gradually took on their colours again. The pines became green, their trunks red; on the branches of the wild roses, the flowers were pink and white. Day was breaking, soon it would be fully broken. You could use your eyes again, and look. You saw that the rocks rose up before you, barring your way. But you also saw that between the rocks there was a narrow aperture.

Maurice Nendaz stops abruptly. He listens, says to Justin, "You hear?"

He leans over the void. Justin, joining him, does the same, and what they hear is that they hear nothing. They no longer hear anything, that is.

The raucous voice that had been speaking five hundred metres below them, at the bottom of the gorge, had fallen silent. Or at least it was in the process of falling silent, having already been terribly weak and intermittent, as if a person being strangled were crying out with less and less strength, less and less.

It was that fissure, that sabre blow that had fallen across the mountain.

Water had long sawed the rock from top to bottom, like the woodcutters who move their serrated blade up and down through the trunk of an oak, one standing on top of it, the other underneath.

Thus it had, over the epochs (ah, what painstaking work!), carved a groove in the walls of rock, which almost touch each other in places, or form overhangs. And in the depths of that groove it continued to flow, no longer seen but making its presence known by a sort of ceaseless sigh that was amplified as it rose through a succession of echoes.

But now that sound of water could no longer be heard; and Nendaz listens and Nendaz says, "Just as I thought."

"The Lizerne?" says Justin.

"Yes."

"What, dammed?"

Nendaz nods, straightens up. As the sky continued to grow lighter, you saw that the path wasn't blocked after all, but that it switched direction sharply behind the opening, continuing, at right angles to itself, to climb the gorge.

It was now almost flat as it traversed the rock. It stretched out before them for quite a way, running parallel to the torrent. At a certain point it crossed a rockslide, then turned another corner and vanished.

Nendaz nods again and sets off. He pushes on to the place where the path turns, where the view opens up to the north. There he points to something in the distance, in the sky: something that has just appeared above a last wooded rise, something yellowish that shines in the morning light, something flat like a plank of pine whose end already extends beyond the surrounding peaks.

"You see?"

Justin indicates that he does.

"You know what it is?"

"No," says Justin.

"You think it's mist, eh? Or smoke? Fog rising? Look closely. Shouldn't smoke curl? And fog is like the shavings from a carpenter's plane. Not that, see how it rises up cleanly, in a straight line? Can you guess…?"

Justin didn't have time to say whether he guessed or not: someone was coming along the path. They noticed the stones rolling toward them before they saw who it was, then they saw. It was a boy of around fourteen, a boy a little younger than Justin, that is. He was brown and grey due to the drawers that stopped just above his shoes and the dirty shirt he was wearing. He ran, then walked a few steps, then ran again. He ran straight towards the two men as if he hadn't seen them. But they had seen him and they also saw that he must have a hole in his head or a wound under his hair, from where the blood had flowed onto his cheek and, mixing with his tears, dried there. Because he was crying, then he wasn't, then a great sob rose into his throat and he ran faster and tried to swallow it.

"You know him?"

"Yes," says Justin. "He's a Donneloye from Premier… His name is Dsozet. He must have come from Zamperon."

So Nendaz opens his arms wide, to block the boy's advance. But was the boy even aware of him, blinded as he was by his tears? He came closer, he didn't stop, he was right on top of Nendaz. Justin was too surprised to act, but Nendaz stepped quickly aside, afraid of being knocked over, given that the drop was sheer at the side of the path.

The boy goes on by.

He is already long past by the time Nendaz says to Justin, "Quick, run, catch him up! You have to get to the village before him. Go to the mayor, you hear, and tell him to come and bring two or three men…"

Justin was off; Nendaz shouted after him, "Tell him it's Derborence. That noise last night, the wind… The smoke… The Devils' Place…"

He shouted, "The devils came down!"

An hour later the stretcher appeared.

Sometimes those from the high chalets use a stretcher to bring down a wounded goat, say, if the goat has had a horn torn off in fighting, or broken a hoof. They tie the goat to the stretcher and cover it with an old cheesecloth. One man carries the front, the other the rear.

You come across them occasionally, like this, on the mountain paths. They come down slowly, putting their right feet forward together, their left feet forward together, so as to keep the stretcher level.

You see them from a distance. You ask yourself, "What are they carrying?" Then a breeze lifts the edge of the cloth, or the animal lifts it itself, by raising its head, and you are reassured by a glimpse of its beard and those odd excrescences under its chin, by its lively, startled eyes and the hoarse bleat that escapes from its muzzle when it opens it, revealing a pink tongue.

They were carrying a stretcher that morning too, and it was covered in a cheese-cloth, but the thing beneath it wasn't a goat. It was heavier, longer than a goat. It was someone, a person, and a person who was too long for the stretcher, such that a part of his body hung down in front. You could see two legs. At the back they had supported his head with a red-and-white checkered pillowcase stuffed with hay, because it was a man that was being carried that morning, and not without difficulty.

There were four to carry him. They took it in turns, a pair at a time. Four of the men from Zamperon, including Biollaz and Loutre. The two who carried the stretcher went ahead while the other two followed, empty-handed.

Every now and then, the ones carrying the stretcher put it down on the path, and the other two took over.

Thus they proceeded along the narrow, tortuous path, taking it in turns, each turn lasting five or six minutes. Four or five hours of that, they had to look forward to, because the path was long. They had to come down the entire length of the gorge, beneath a ribbon of sky that was barely any wider or less tortuous. They took it in turns, two by two, their arms flexed, their shoulders drooping, a vein as fat as a finger bulging in their extended necks, taking care to put the same foot forward at the same time – five or six minutes each, and then they stopped.

The four of them surrounded the stretcher. They said, "Hey, Barthelémy!"

They shook their heads.

"He can't hear us."

One of them tore a handful of grass from the side of the path and, leaning over the patient, clumsily wiped away the foam at the corners of his mouth, giving him a pink beard within his own beard, a pink beard full of bubbles as when you blow through a straw into soapy water.

The man offered no resistance. He didn't move or speak, just stared at the sky with empty, unseeing eyes. His eyes were wide open but blank, as if his gaze had turned inward. He had a pink beard above his neat, black beard. He had a large face that had been tanned and ruddy with good health and the outdoors life, but which was now grey and green, like a stone that has rolled in moss and been first worn by it and then polished, because his complexion which appeared dusty in places was shiny in others, where the skin was stretched over the skull. All of a sudden Barthelémy's breathing came shorter, faster, it expelled a new wave of froth, because his chest had been crushed, and they were taking him down to the village to try to save him.

Having put him down on the path, the men called him, shaking their heads beneath the narrow sky, in the gorge that lay in shadow even on the sunniest day. They said, "Are you thirsty, Barthelémy?", one of them having taken a horn cup from his pocket and filled it from a rivulet that trickled by the side of the path. He leaned over, but the water ran down Barthelémy's chin, it streamed over his mouth which no longer understood, which refused, which said no.

They set off again. They saw Nendaz coming towards them.

He had pushed on into the gorge with his bad leg and his cane, and had thus covered part of the distance. They had covered the rest.

The two who were unencumbered had moved in front. Nendaz said to them, "Is it the mountain?"

The two men nodded.

Nendaz said, "I knew it… last night… So," he said, indicating the stretcher, "he's the only one left?"

The two men nodded.

"Of all those who went up?"

"Yes."

"And at Zamperon?"

"One has a broken arm. He'll be along soon, we fixed him up with a bandage."

Nendaz took off his hat and crossed himself. They did the same.

Then they said, "Down there, do they know?"

"No, they think it was a storm."

"Ah! They don't know?"

"By now they probably know," said Nendaz, "because one of your kids just came by, and I sent Justin to warn them."

The ones carrying the stretcher caught up with them.

Nendaz said, "Who is it?"

"Barthelémy."

"Ah!" said Nendaz, "Barthelémy…"

He took a step forward, hat in hand.

"Barthelémy, Barthelémy, it's me. It's me, Maurice Nendaz… Do you hear me? Hey, Barthelémy!"

VI

Philomène woke early with the feeling that something pleasant had happened to her the previous evening. And indeed it was a pleasant thing, she thought as the first grey ash of morning insinuated itself through the half-closed shutters of the bedroom: the promise of a child. The idea that you are going to be a grandmother is a pleasant thing. A child arrives and everything falls into place.

Her thoughts fell into place as she dressed. She said to herself, "From the moment they wed, in fact…" She said to herself, "And then, from the moment things turned out well." Because a child on the way is things turning out well. They were going to need her, and for an old woman that meant a new lease of life, an idea that hadn't escaped her either, and that made her feel happy and warm, on this side of the windows, while the day broke on the other.

She continued to cogitate and now her mind turned to Thérèse. "I shouldn't have let her go last night. What was I thinking? I should have kept her here with me, because you're always a bit jittery to begin with."

But then she thought, "Well, I'll go quickly and make the soup and take her some piping hot under a cloth so that she can eat it in bed… It'll do her good to have a lie-in."

A byre door opens, someone is off to milk a goat. There are almost no cows left in the village in summer, and no able men either: it's a village of goats, women, children and old people. Someone pulls on a rusty bolt that squeals like a stuck pig. Someone coughs. The fountain is made of a tree trunk sawn in half and hollowed out; it's old Jean Carrupt who's coughing. So bearded in moss is the fountain, that from far away you can barely distinguish it from the grassy bank behind it. Instead of a pipe feeding it, there's a simple wooden channel that's cracked along its length, so that half the water leaks away before it reaches the basin. Old Jean Carrupt is up with the lark and he's always thirsty. Besides, they're practically all Carrupts in the village, so they tell each other apart by their first names and nicknames.

Jean Carrupt had been to drink at the fountain. Returning, he dragged his feet.

Philomène had lit the fire, she had hung the pot over it. People were beginning to come and go beneath the windows, bathed in a pretty pink colour that had started in the sky to the east and now suffused everything.

Old Carrupt's back was pink beneath the tailcoat that he had worn for more than twenty years.

He turns his back, heading for the slope that rises above the village.

Time passes.

Suddenly, old Carrupt mutters something.

A woman says to him, "What's that, Father Jean?"

He mutters again.

"Well I never, so it is! Hey, Marie, d'you see? On the path?"

"Who is it?"

"I don't know."

"What are they up to?"

"Oh kids, having fun…"

It was the two boys, they were on the path and they seemed to be playing tag. One ran, the other ran. Dsozet was in front, Justin behind. When the one behind ran faster, the one in front did the same, as if to avoid being caught. Because in tag, the game is to catch the other, and he who catches wins.

The women watched.

"Where are they going?"

"Why are they running?"

They saw that despite Dsozet's best efforts, the gap between the two was shrinking. And in fact, when Justin sped up again, he came level with Dsozet. The women were surprised, because rather than tap him on the shoulder or tackle him, as they had expected, he simply ran on by without saying a word to Dsozet, without even glancing at him.

"It's Justin. But where has he come from? I know he was here last night."

"Sure, I saw him."

This is how misfortune arrives, on two legs, or two times two legs, though we don't recognise it. This is how bad news approaches and moves on, quickly, before we suspect it. The women call Justin, because by now he's close.

"Hey, Justin!"

He doesn't answer. He leaves the path and heads off across the gardens, as if to avoid being questioned. As for little Dsozet, he had vanished, having taken the road for Premier without even entering the village.

Hearing the women's voices, Philomène has come out onto her doorstep. She spots them moving between the houses, trying to see where Justin is headed. He's obviously searching for someone. Finally he stops in front of the mayor's house, which is right at the other end of the village, next to the one where, in a room on the first floor that is reached by a wooden staircase as steep as a ladder, Rebord serves drink.

Justin enters the mayor's house, he emerges with the mayor, and misfortune is upon us. Because Justin reappears. Justin comes out of the mayor's house, he raises his arm, he points to the north. Justin gestures with both arms, then with just one of them he indicates the mountains again. The mayor nods. The mayor looks around, moves forward. He's a little old man with a white moustache; his name is Crettenand. He raises his hand to his white moustache, strokes it; then shrugs his shoulders brusquely. They remain momentarily hunched at his ears. All around is silence in which a cock's crow echoes mockingly, then Rebord clatters down his steps.

He makes a noise like a drumroll.

A man's voice says, "It's not true!"

Then a woman: "Ah…! Ah…! Ah…!"

A long cry that comes in three waves, each more shrill than the last, before breaking at its weakest point like a reed in the wind.

The village begins to stir as people run toward Justin and the mayor.

"The mountain?"

"Yes."

"You mean…? On Derborence…? It's not possible, what are you saying?"

"Remember the noise last night?"

People weep, women call out, children shout. They converge shoving each other, pushing and shoving in the alley. Misfortune is upon us and at long last we recognise it, because four or five men are standing around the mayor.

There were women who laughed, saying, "Come on, it isn't true…"

The mayor said, "Who knows, let me through, we have to go see…"

Philomène had come too. She slipped between the women, she worked her way between the raised arms and the shaking heads.

"So," she said, "what's this all about, Mayor…?"

He comes forward, says, "I don't know, ask Justin."

"Well," she says to Justin, "what about Séraphin?"

"Don't know."

"And Antoine?"

"Don't know."

She sets off at a run towards Thérèse's house where nothing seems to have stirred yet, because it is quite a way from the commotion. She sees that the door to the house is unlocked.

She knocks at the bedroom door.

"Is that you, Mother?"

She says, "It's me."

She enters. She says, "You left the windows open, you'll catch cold…"

Quickly she shuts the windows.

"You must look after yourself, you know, in your condition… Did you sleep well? Oh, I woke you… Never mind! I was worried about you, that's why I came."

Almost no sound penetrates the windows with their glass as thick as the heel of a bottle.

She takes a long time to rearrange the little curtains that the night's wind had disturbed. She says, "Stay in bed this morning, just to be on the safe side. I'll bring you your soup."

She hasn't turned round yet. She hears Thérèse say, "Oh no, I'll get up."

"You're feeling better then?"

Yes," said Thérèse, "much better!"

Suddenly a cry penetrates the walls and the thick glass, someone is running past the house.

"What's that?"

"Nothing," says Philomène.

"But… What's the matter with you, Mother?"

Because Philomène had to turn around sooner or later, and now she presents to her daughter a face the colour of dirty paper, as she clasps her hands over her belt to still them.

And even though she's standing in shadow, Thérèse stares at her, because you can't stop the truth from getting out.

"Nothing's the matter."

Thérèse says, "That's odd."

She's sitting on the bed.

Someone knocks at the door of the house.

Thérèse hears her mother and another woman speaking in low voices in the kitchen. She can't hear what they're saying. Meanwhile, outside, the noise grows louder and louder as it comes closer and closer. Once again Thérèse asks, "What's going on?"

The two women came in, the other being Catherine, one of Philomène's sisters.

"Don't pay any attention," said Catherine. "It's Barthelémy's wife, she's upset… Her little one is sick."

They were still standing by the door, the two of them, ill at ease but trying to appear calm, wanting to come closer but held back, looking for words but finding none.

Philomène's hands twitched more and more violently against her striped apron.

"Wait," said Thérèse, "I'm coming, I'm getting up."

"No," said Catherine, "it's better if you stay in bed."

Just then a bell was struck; once, then again, and again.

Barthelémy had died. The men carrying him saw that he was dead because his mouth had fallen open in his beard.

They were almost at the village. They put the stretcher down on the path. Then, bareheaded, they stood around him, the four of them and Nendaz, and then all those who had come up to meet them (which was why the noise had receded): the mayor, Justin, Rebord, men, women, children.

The women fell to their knees and someone set off at a run for the chapel.

The bell was struck.

Thérèse said, "Who's dead?"

"Oh," said Catherine (then ran out of words)... "It's Barthelémy's wife's little one, merciful god. That's right, it must be him... Ah, poor woman!"

Another strike. Thérèse said, "He wasn't sick yesterday."

"That's right, Barthelémy's wife's little one... She said he had croup... It came on last night."

The bell was struck again.

"She ran around the houses like a madwoman... As if there was anything we could do, the rest of us..."

And again. In the other place, the women got to their feet. The porters took up their load again, one at each end. They pulled the cheesecloth over the dead man's face.

Peace lies over the mountains that are arranged in a half-circle high up in the sky. From the place the dead man quits, we have a view over the village. We see, beyond the rooftops, the void of the valley filled, this morning, with a soft mist in which the colour of the sun and that of the shade are sewn together like the bands of a flag. Higher up it's lighter, and the higher you look the lighter it is. They glow tranquilly, those towers, those horns, those needles, all in gold or all in silver, and they quiver like the flame of a candle in church when someone passes by.

All is peaceful on the mountains, all is rest, but for me, there will never be rest again.

Barthelémy quits his place. He's made to quit it, he doesn't resist, he lets it happen. He descends a little further. The others follow. They don't dare weep any more, they no longer dare even speak. They have silenced their tears which now flow noiselessly down their cheeks.

Rest. But for me there will never be rest again, no never again, in this life.

Because her mother and her aunt had tried to stop her, but they hadn't had the strength. Thérèse runs across the bedroom to the window, she sees. First there's Barthelémy who's being carried; a man is at his feet, a man is at his head and he's on his back. They're upright, he's laid out; they're walking, he's still, passive under his cloth. His feet come first, spilling over the front of the stretcher, followed by the rise which is his head on the pillow.

Tranquillity, rest. He comes like this and after him comes the crowd.

Old Carrupt goes to meet them. He doesn't quite grasp what's going on; now and then he lets out a little grunt.

"That's nice," says Thérèse. "Something bad happens and I'm the last one to know."

Her mother and her aunt try to pull her away, but here comes Barthelémy's wife with her six children.

The bell continues to ring out. One strike, then another, then another. The bell is struck and Barthelémy's wife holds the smallest child against her, taking the hand of another who is barely walking, while two more cling to the back of her skirt.

She has six children.

There's Nendaz with his cane. Thérèse recognises Nendaz.

He's coming closer.

He is a face among all the other faces that float just above the ground, at the level of the little windows that form a line low down in the brown wooden walls – bearded or cleanshaven, hair mussed or shorn, or else long for the women and knotted in buns, brunette, black, blonde...

"Very nice!"

Then to Nendaz: "Heavens, what's happening?"

Because Barthelémy is passing beneath the window, on his back, his face covered. From above she sees the full length of him, sees that he isn't moving. Then his wife begins to sob again, letting her tears flow down her face and into her mouth. They form black stains against her grey blouse.

Arms are raised, hands pressed to each side of a head. The men, on the other hand, lower theirs: the mayor, Justin, Rebord, Nendaz, the others – there aren't many of them, and alas, that's the way it'll stay! Not many because of all the deaths up there. It's a small village, a village of goats, women, children, old people. All this time he is coming, now he is underneath Thérèse and she says, "What happened?"

She is still talking about Barthelémy. She says, "I think he's dead. Is it true, Maurice Nendaz?"

Nendaz passes with his cane.

"Why doesn't he answer? Odd," she says. "What's the matter with them? Justin!"

Justin seems not to have heard, he passes too, he's already past.

A woman looks up at Thérèse.

"Don't you know? You still don't know...? My god!"

She falls silent without finishing her sentence.

It's as if she has already forgotten Thérèse. The bell is struck.

"Come away from the window," says Philomène. "You'll catch cold. We'll explain…"

And Thérèse: "Explain what?"

But she already has her explanation because another woman says, "The mountain fell down."

"What mountain?"

"The Devils' Place."

"Fell down where?"

"On Derborence."

Thérèse says, "And them?"

But she bursts out laughing: "The mountain!"

Again, laughing: "A mountain doesn't just fall down!"

Then suddenly: "Where's Antoine?"

She cries out, "My husband! Oh Antoine, my love!"

They later calculated the volume of the landslide to be more than a hundred and fifty million cubic feet. A hundred and fifty million cubic feet, that makes some noise when it comes down. And it did make a lot of noise, noise that was heard throughout the valley, which is a league or two wide and at least fifteen long. It's just that at first, nobody knew what the noise meant.

They were about to find out because the news travelled fast, even though there was neither telegraph nor telephone nor cars. It's soon said. You say, "The mountain's fallen down."

Thanks to little Dsozet, the news reached Premier around the same time that it reached Aïre. He stood by the fountain while they washed the blood off his face. Blurted from his mouth, the news ran from house to house.

Above you, a white brilliance flickers in the sky that arcs down to meet you like the vaulted roof of a cellar. Beneath it, the news spreads.

At first it keeps to the path, then it veers off it.

It runs straight down, leaping over hedges.

A man repairing the aqueduct raises his head. "What's that?" "The mountain..." "What mountain?"

And the geckos, sunning themselves on the scree, slink back into their holes.

"Derborence..."

The news runs and runs, heading for the great valley which suddenly opens up there in two colours between the pines. It skitters across the scarp and tumbles through the vines to the Rhone which hits you full in the face with its white fire.

There's a small town there where a doctor mounts his horse around eleven each morning, having attached his medicine bag to the saddle behind him.

Before noon the news reaches the county town, where the government sits, causing uproar in the cafés.

They drink the local muscat there.

"Derborence!"

A wine so golden it's verging on brown; a wine that warms the palate with its rough taste, while its bouquet climbs from the back of the mouth to fill the nose.

They said, "Not a single one left alive, apparently."

"And the cows?"

"Not one!"

They came to the threshold and looked up, but from where they stood, relative to the mountains, they couldn't see a thing. Nothing at all. At most, way up high to the west, a greyish wisp of cloud, as transparent as muslin, stretched out flat in the sky behind the rocks.

Until about six in the evening there was hardly anybody up there besides the inhabitants of Zamperon. Those who had stayed, that is, which is to say not many. Not more than five or six, of whom one was a woman. Having put the cows to graze close to the chalets, so as not to have to watch over them, they had taken up their hammers and picks and set about trying to open a door that had jammed, or nail down any roof tiles that had come loose.

And it was then that two men from Anzeindaz appeared. They had made a long detour via the high places to avoid having to pass too close to the rockfall.

They came. At first they said nothing. They came and they said nothing. They watched the ones from Zamperon who said nothing either, then they nodded.

"So?"

"Yes," said the ones from Zamperon, and they nodded in turn.

"What a calamity!" said the ones from Anzeindaz. "Did any come out alive?"

"One."

"One?"

"That's all! And he's not in a good way. They've just taken him down."

They understood each other with difficulty, not speaking the same patois. But the ones from Anzeindaz spoke up again.

"We came to see if you needed a hand. We could send a team."

Those from Zamperon replied, "Thanks, but as you see, we're managing."

They pointed to the crater where Derborence once lay: "As for them…"

They let their hands fall.

"They don't need anyone any more."

They sat together, for a moment, on a stretch of wall in the sun, and drank the eau-de-vie that the men from Anzeindaz had brought in a bag with some clothes.

Meanwhile, the Germans from Sanetsch came down too, looking for news. They appeared suspended above one another, as if on a rope ladder, in the flues of the Woodcarrier's Passage; first visible, then invisible, then once again hoving into view, according to whether the white cloud that floated there against the rockface enveloped them or set them free.

They came, and these ones, speaking only German, tried to make themselves understood by means of gestures. Thus the men from three countries came together, briefly, to drink eau-de-vie, because it's at Derborence that the frontiers of these three countries meet; the ones from Anzeindaz coming from the west, the ones from Sanetsch from the northeast.

Seated side-by-side, they passed the cup between them, looking across the stream to the shoulder of mountain where the forest of young pines had once stood. The trees now lay on the ground, lined up in the direction the wind had blown them, some torn up by the roots, others snapped in half, as when a person tries cutting wheat with a blunt scythe at harvest time.

Each had something to say in his own tongue.

They passed the cup, they looked towards the stream, they saw that the big stones that littered the bed had almost dried out, leaving pools stranded between them, pools filled with silence, pools that shone like eye glasses. Their ears strained to catch the rush of the torrent there where it should have been but no longer was, and in the air around them, and they marvelled at the fact of this new silence.

One by one they stopped talking, and then those from Sanetsch and those from Anzeindaz set off back to where they had come from.

Aïre, on the other hand, was bustling. They had come up as soon as they had had heard, the priest and many of the people of Premier, because Premier was the main village in the parish.

The doctor arrived a little after noon, his horse in a lather.

There was also a broken arm; it belonged to a young man of around twenty named Placide Fellay. He sat in a kitchen while the doctor, having produced splints and bandages, set the fracture.

One man held him by the shoulders and another by the legs.

As for the dead man, it was simply a case of verifying that he was dead: this twenty-third of June. People kept coming. The doctor leaned over the bed where they had lain Barthelémy to listen to his heart: where once there had been a heartbeat, now there was only silence.

The surface of a mirror placed in front of Barthelémy's mouth (having first been rubbed against a knee) remained unclouded.

The doctor straightened up, shook his head. Then: "Agh…"

A long moan, then another and then a third. It was carried as far as the street where, stopping, they said to one another, "That's Barthelémy's wife."

Meanwhile the police had arrived, and the doctor was getting ready to leave for Derborence with two or three men and a mule loaded with provisions.

They questioned Biollaz, but all he said was, "You'll see."

Loutre was with him. Biollaz said, "Blocks, blocks bigger than…"

He indicated the houses.

"Two or three times bigger than our buildings, they dammed the stream… The Lizerne… They covered the pastures… What do you suppose could have stood up to that?"

They asked, "And Barthelémy?"

"Oh," said Biollaz, "it's because his chalet was set a little apart, above the others… But he was caught in it anyway, as you saw. And it would have been better for the poor beggar if it had killed him outright…"

They asked him, "How many?"

"Nineteen, all told… fifteen from Aïre and four from Premier…"

"And cows…?"

"Good god, at least a hundred and fifty… And then there were the goats…"

By now the mule was ready, and the men set off without further delay.

And now it shifts to this house, this other house. Here, here again, but also there and a little further away too. Over there, someone's laughing. They say it's the wife of the dead man, laughing because she's lost her mind.

By now strangers are passing constantly in front of your house: they stop, they look, they shake their heads.

Old Jean Carrupt, who hasn't really grasped what's going on, walks on. From time to time he too comes to a halt and mutters something to himself.

It's in ten or twelve houses, the misfortune, here and again here and over there, and all the while people stop and stare, and you hear voices, screams, moaning, then nothing. You hear laughing and at the same time weeping.

The rockfall at Derborence, one twenty-third of June – only ten days after they went up.

"If only they'd waited…" they said.

"Why would they? It was time. They went up when they always do."

"Me," she said, "I don't believe any of it."

They had made Thérèse go back to bed. Her mother and her aunt had stayed with her.

People kept knocking at the door.

"Don't come in," said Catherine to them. "Please, leave her alone."

They passed in front of the house: "Two in that house… a brother and a husband… the mother's brother, the daughter's husband…"

"Antoine Pont."

"And Séraphin Carrupt."

So the dead acquired names and were slowly counted. And when they opened the door, they saw the reflection at the top of the stairwell of the fire burning on the kitchen range.

Apparently she was expecting a child.

Water was being heated in the pot over the stove and she, in her bed: "Does a mountain fall down just like that? Don't make me laugh."

She became agitated. Thinking she had a fever, they put a cold compress on her forehead.

"If mountains fall down just like that, what are we going to do? We're not short of mountains, around here…"

She said, "Take this compress away."

Then Philomène, swallowing her tears: "Oh please, Thérèse, please!"

And Thérèse: "Leave me be. I'm fine."

"But it's not just about you."

"Who then?"

She stops moving, thinks.

Suddenly she asks, "What's that noise?"

"People."

She said, "What people?"

"People wanting news."

"Oh!" she said. "In that case, it must be true... If there are people... The mountain... Oh!" And addressing her mother: "What about you, do you think he's dead?"

"We don't know yet. We'll have to wait and see. Nobody knows anything; they've only just left."

"Who?"

"The doctor and the police."

"So we have to wait. But how long?"

"Until tomorrow or the day after. We promise to tell you everything."

"No need."

She said, "Why are they bothering?"

She says, "Couldn't I go with them?"

She sat up and the two women ran to the bed, each one seizing her by a shoulder and pushing her back down.

"What good would it do? Wait, child. Do as we do. How can we help, eh? What difference would it make?"

Tears ran down the old woman's cheeks.

"You must think of him, too."

"Who?"

"Him, the little one who's on his way."

"Fine!"

She puts herself in their hands, allows herself to be laid back, lies still, once again, on her pillow. She crosses her hands on the sheet. The mountains will soon turn pink. The mountains fall on us. They're beautiful to look at, but they're dangerous.

"What if I have a child? What if I have Antoine's child? He's not coming back, I know that. But then this little baby, he'll be an orphan, an orphan before he's born... Ah," she said, "Antoine would have been so happy! I would have whispered the secret in his ear... Oh well, I won't be telling him anything now. He'll never know. How strange."

Suddenly she cried out, "Well I don't want it... I don't want it! A child without a father, is it still a child? Oh, take it away, take it away, take it away!"

PART TWO

I

He stuck out his head…

It was almost two months since the rockfall, so they had had plenty of time to measure it, having got out their rubberised measuring tape for the purpose, on which the units were ticked off by black lines, and having held it first longways, then widthways, taut against the rocks. Then one of the men climbed as high as he could inside the section of fall that appeared the most elevated, to try to gauge the thickness of the mass. He was an employee of the land registry, because they made the pilgrimage to Derborence too, following in the footsteps of the medics, the police and the curious.

A hundred and fifty million cubic feet. They quantified the landslide so as to be able to alter the plans of the commune, and to work out which areas, once designated pasture and fertile land, should now be labelled unfit for use.

It was a daunting task, but those who undertook it had plenty of time to do a thorough job. There was nothing to distract them, because the curious became fewer and fewer as the days passed, and nature left them to it, having retreated to a state of calm, having resumed her habitual stillness, having settled back into indifference. Finally some gentlemen from town climbed up onto the glacier and walked up and down it, looking for new crevices that might have opened up behind the break-point and that might pose, if not an imminent danger, then at least a future risk. But everything appeared to be in order, they found no tears in that pristine sheet which, smooth and white, covered the flattish space behind the ridge from one side to the other.

Now that the dust cloud had inched its way higher than the walls of rock, the bottom of the Derborence crater was visible again. The air, once opaque, had become limpid. Those who made it that far had only to lift their heads to see, at the bottom of the sky, the point were the slide had started. It was a place where the rockface had previously jutted out under a mass of ice that bristled with spines, vestiges of ancient glaciers that, in this part of the world, we call seracs. What had stood out in relief was now hollow, what had been convex was now concave. The rocky projection had been replaced by a vast chute that plummeted downwards. This chute had discharged its contents in one fell swoop onto the pastures, so that they had ceased to be pastures, on those who had inhabited them, so that they had ceased to inhabit them, on those who had lived there and who lived no more. Nothing remained but the stillness and tranquillity of death. The only thing that still moved up there was a muddy mass, a river of sand, earth and water that continued to pour from the mouth of the chute. But reined in by those walls of rock, channelled by them, it cascaded soundlessly onto the cone of refuse that broke its fall. That silent displacement of the landscape barely grazed the senses, so that you had to watch for a long time to discern it.

A collection had been made in the region, to compensate those who had lost their animals in the disaster, at least in part. The commune had also ceded parcels of its own pasture to those who had been affected, to replace the ones they had lost at Derborence.

Aside from that, all that remained was to make a slight adjustment to the map; to add a simple footnote to the relevant page of the register. The question was raised as to whether that particular page shouldn't be redrawn, since it was coloured green. And green means grass, which means life.

Nothing left up there but old Plan with his flock of sheep that roamed the ravines like the shadow of a cloud.

The flock has to keep moving. Nothing grows in those empty places, except for a thin tuft of grass in the cracks between rocks, like the weeds that sprout between the paving stones of a courtyard. It harvests each precious blade. It advances, grazing as it goes. It's on the move from dawn 'til dusk, square, spear-shaped, sometimes assuming a triangular form, sometimes a rectangular one, sometimes on the slopes, sometimes in the depths of a gorge, mimicking the shadow of a cloud whose shape shifts as the wind toys with it in the air above you. It moves forward, it curls one way around a hill, the other way around a dell. It becomes convex, then concave. Its hooves make a noise like rain; its teeth, the one that wavelets make when they lap the pebbles of the shore.

As for him, he stood close by, rooted to the earth like an old larch in winter.

Rooted there, upright, immobile in his greatcoat, his white beard bobbing under his old hat with its frayed rim.

"D… D… E…"

He laughed.

"Nobody left… Nobody left? Are you sure…?"

He said, "The surveyors went away, they were wise… But just because they left, doesn't mean…"

CHAPTER I

He repeated, "D… E… DE… V…"

Just then a stone falling with the river of mud struck the fallen mountain with a sound like laughter.

"I see that you understand me."

And the great mass of rock shook with mirth as the sound splintered and detonated to right and left, until very soon the peels of laughter merged into a single hum. The mountain was laughing and he replied, "I see there's no need for me to go on, you know your own name…"

The mountain fell quiet. It resumed its silence, he waited his turn.

"You know… I know, and so do you," he said to the mountain. "You, you're just the middle man. But the one who pulls the strings, you know who he is, don't you? D… E… V… I… And you hear them too, at night, poor souls, the ones he's holding hostage. At night, when I'm hunkered down in my bothy and you, you're way up high, you hear them too, eh? They weep and moan, because they can find no rest. They look like men, but they're empty, nothing but husks. But we hear them at night, and we see them too, don't we…?"

The mountain started laughing again.

And out popped that head, but nobody saw it because of the rocks that protruded, that surrounded it, that shielded it from view on all sides.

II

He sticks out his head.

It is almost two months since the rockslide.

To see him you'd have to have the eyes and wings of the eagle that soars overhead, scanning the earth with its piercing, meticulous gaze, picking out in a heartbeat that which lives from that which doesn't, that which stirs from that which is immobile, that which is animate from that which is inert. Being high above everything, that small, grey eye, for which distance is nothing, is able to discern the merest movement, the merest displacement of being or thing, hares dancing, or the baby marmot emerging from its burrow.

As for him, nobody saw him, tiny as he was, lost in that vast desert of stone.

Only the eagle could have spied him, because of that head that moved against the stone that didn't. When the eagle wheels slowly, keeping its wings steady, tipping them a little more, a little less, according to the direction of the wind and the air pressure, just as fishermen do their sails, then it banks one way, it banks the other, it goes, it returns, all the while dominating from a great height that vast caving-in where the immense blocks amount to nothing more than a smattering of gravel.

It was there that this head showed itself. There in the bright sun that, for two hours, had shone down from above the chain of mountains; in a tiny stain of shadow like a drop of ink that has fallen onto grey blotting paper.

You'd have seen him from up there, but it was only from up there that he could have been seen, when at first he stuck out his head and the rest of him had yet to emerge.

If only one could say to the eagle: "Lose a little altitude, go down and get a better look. Leave these dizzy heights, fall."

But he hangs there, hesitating, because man is not his prey and he's afraid of man.

And yet it's a poor man that erupts from the earth, a poor man who appears in a gap the blocks left between them during their haphazard fall. A man come out of the shadows, come out of who knows what depths, come out of the night, pushing up toward the light.

He forms a lighter stain against the semi-darkness that surrounds him. He is white-skinned with white shoulders. He sticks out his head, lifts it up.

He must realise that he can't see anything from there.

Nothing but the blue of the sky when he looks up; a smooth, flat sky, cut in a round, taut as the disk of paper stretched over a jam jar.

He has to raise himself up a little higher on his hands and knees, inside the fault that contains him and that grows wider towards the top. Not all of him can be seen because he's in shadow, but then his head reaches the edge of the sunlight.

The sun strikes his head.

He stops again.

His hair is long, down to his nape.

With his two hands he parts it in front of his eyes, pushing it back behind his ears where it sticks like wet sheets.

He bats his eyelids. He closes his eyes, opens them, closes them again.

He's lost the habit of sunlight and he has to learn it again, because it's beautiful, sunlight, but it can harm you. It's good, but it burns.

It's like when you give a small child eau-de-vie: the blood rushes in his ears, but he can't tell if the buzzing is on the inside or the outside, having forgotten how to hear, how to see, the pleasure of colours, having lost taste, smell and the ability to recognise forms or judge distances.

He closes his eyes, he opens his eyes. He sticks his fingers in his ears and shakes his head like a dog coming out of the water. And little by little, the sweetness of life works its magic, whispering to him with its sunshine, its colours, all its goodness, and he feels as if his body were wrapped in warm clothes.

He takes a great gulp of air.

It has a taste and a perfume, it descends through his body, it flows into his stomach and around his belly, invigorating him. Now he raises himself a little higher between the two masses of rock either side of him, that are half-covered in scree, until he reaches their upper surfaces, and from there the view opens up on all sides.

He stretches out on the rock.

His entire body is in the sun now, once again he's under the influence of the star and dependent on it. All this space! At last, more than he could possibly need!

He stretches his legs and yawns. He raises his arms above his head, then lowers them so that they extend outwards from his body. He doesn't come into contact with anything. All he touches is air which is soft, elastic, which gives way immediately, then flows back.

How good it feels! "Ah!" he says to himself. "That's good!" He yawns. He scratches his head, his neck, his back, his thighs. He's visible now, all of him can be seen, he's the colour of turnips. His toes stick out from what's left of his boots. One leg of his trousers stops at the knee; the other is ripped down the side. He feels good, he yawns again, he shifts onto the other elbow. He's got on a sort of jacket that is torn at the back right up to the shoulder blades. Wide open in front, it reveals his gaunt chest and the beard on his chin.

From the tips of his toes to the crown of his head, he is one single colour, and the colour continues to change, rapidly, becoming ever lighter: the leather, the cloth, his own skin, his hair, all has been repainted a shade of grey that is turning to white.

He's found in his pocket an old crust of black bread that he must have slipped in there deliberately. With both hands he holds it up to his mouth, and the sound he makes with his teeth can be heard all around.

The flies gather; butterflies come too, little white ones, others a delicate grey and blue, rising and falling, suspended in the air like confetti. He eats ravenously, swallowing his saliva, inside the little black cloud that envelopes him.

Now he looks around, he sees. Objects place themselves in front of other objects; distance, greater or lesser, opens up between them. Space arranges itself around him, vertically and in depth. The sun helps it. The sun would like to prevent it, but it fails. The man forces the sun to help: if you don't want to, I'll make you. That's a stone, and that's another stone. He sees splintered rocks whose bared inner surface is now exposed to the light: blues with veins of white, violets like periwinkles, chestnut browns, others the colour of the clover flower or blackened as if by fire. As many stones as you could wish for, and superposed and juxtaposed as they are, they create something unreal. But the sun is on them, and the sun is real.

It exists, he says to himself. I exist. But where am I?

He sees that he is in the middle of a vast desert of stones; he tries, with a great effort, to organise his thoughts.

And on the far side of a long night (but did I stay put, or did I move from place to place, wandering beneath the earth until, who knows how long it went on for, I passed clean under the mountain?), on the far side of a long night, he rediscovers the same sun, but a sun that, he knows, once illuminated abundant green grass, rich pasture scattered with cows, where men spread manure. Everything was alive, the bells tinkled around the cows' necks, men called each other – silence. He looks: no more men, no more cows, no more grass, no more chalets. He sees stones and more stones and still more stones. He sees a vast field of stones that slopes gently down toward the other range, the one that rises to the south. He knows that range well, but the thing shining at his feet he doesn't recognise to begin with. It's water; two small lakes.

They weren't there before. Where am I?

He scratches his head again.

Each time he makes a movement the flies that cover him take off with a noise like a plucked violin string. He must be at Derborence, he thinks. That's where I am, I know that's where I am. The lower reaches have changed, but the peaks are the same. Down here everything's different, up there it's as it was. He names the summits one by one, because the names come back to him: up there is the Peg, here's the tip of the Comb, down there's the gorge and Zamperon, to the left is the Woodcarrier's. And turning a little, he tips his head back and laughs.

He has understood.

He turns to face the north. Something like fifteen hundred metres up, under Saint-Martin, is the cut face of the glacier. He sees the place where it broke; the fracture gleams, still fresh.

He understands. He says to himself, "I see."

He nods. "That's it, I get it, the mountain fell down."

It fell down on top of us, I remember the noise it made and how the roof was flattened on one side.

My god, you can see exactly what path it took! What an avalanche, and from right up high. You can see exactly how it came, straight down, straight for us, as if it had taken aim. Not a house left, obviously – his eye strays over the vast expanse of debris around him, since he is roughly in the middle of it – not a blade of grass, no men, no cows either.

"Where are they?" he says to himself. Then: "They must have got away."

"I got caught under it," he thinks.

"Well I got myself out, it took time, but I got out."

And he feels happy, because he's alive. He has eyes to see, a mouth to breathe, a body (he feels it all over) to carry him where he wants, how he wants, as far as he wants.

His voice seems to be coming back to him. No sooner has he thought the words than they form themselves on his tongue, with sound. It's a voice that runs ahead of him, though, like a dog announcing his master's arrival.

He concocts a sound in his throat, pushes it out. It's shrill and formless, but he hears himself, he hears his own voice. With that first cry, which is sent back to him in an echo, he proves to himself that he exists.

"Oh!"

"O," comes the reply.

Then: "It's me."

"It's you?"

"Yes it's me, Antoine Pont."

He pronounces his name, he repeats it, he says, "The mountain fell down. The mountain fell down on top of me, see, but I got out."

He laughs. The laughter is reciprocated.

He says, "You find that funny, eh? Me too. Where are you?"

He gets up.

It must have been around ten, because the sun was already quite high in the sky. It doesn't show itself until fairly late in these parts, having plodded up behind the range to the east, from slope to slope, to reach the crest.

The sun shone white and round at a good distance from the ridge of rock that blocked the line of sight to the east. It was getting hot, hot enough, even, to burn.

Antoine looked once more to left and right, then turning towards the mouth of the gorge, started to make his way over the rocks in that direction.

They were of different sizes and very unevenly distributed, one boulder having sometimes driven itself between two others. There were rocks that had been trapped upright, like that, so that they towered over the flock like the shepherd over his sheep. There were angular, pointed ones, round ones, slender ones half buried in gravel and sand. In some places they joined up into a sort of continuous floor, in others they were widely spaced with large cracks or gaping holes between them.

He set off cautiously, but laughing with pleasure. At times he slid on his backside, at others, because of his ruined shoes, he carefully chose the spot where he would place his foot before venturing to take a step.

He wasn't far from the lower limit of the slide, at the level of one of the little lakes that had formed behind that barrage. The water now spilled out of the ends of these, forming waterfalls that vanished immediately back into the rocks.

He gazed at this water with admiration, because it was as if the upside-down mountain were sporting at its summit, that's to say down in the depths, a scrap of blue sky, like a sheet left on the line on wash day.

He laughs out loud. "Now what?" he says. "Ah! But there's no-one left. Ho! Hey! Hohey!"

He cups his hands around his mouth and makes the cry of the mountains: "Hohey...!" Nothing but a muted echo comes back, from somewhere among the rocks far behind him.

"Hey! Where is everyone? Hey, can anyone hear me? It's me, Antoine Pont. Hohey! Antoine..."

Nothing.

He starts laughing.

"They've given up on me."

He shouts at the top of his voice, "That's right, it's me... The mountain fell down on me but I got out. It's true!"

Nothing.

"Fine," he shouts. "I'm coming."

And he turned toward the biggest of the boulders, which were also the ones that had rolled the farthest. Turf sprouted in the intervals between them, a bright green turf that carpeted those alleyways. Because they were real alleyways: winding, intersecting, some forming culs-de-sac, others partlally obstructed hallway along. You could lose yourself easily in that multitude and confusion of passages.

It took him a while to find his way through it, but his good mood kept him going.

And abruptly he emerged at the place where the path began again, with its mule tracks and its traces of hobnailed boots left in the mud. Ah, the old footpath, he recognised it!

It ran alongside the stream where the stream rejoined its old bed.

He's back among the familiar. The same water, the same quantity of water, the same colour, leaping over the same stones.

He sees the old path, the path used since ancient times, stretching out in front of him. All he has to do is follow it. Easy! There's no longer anything to impede his progress, and the first barberry bushes and pines are already visible, the former growing at the edge of the path, the latter dotted about on the escarpments to left and right. Easy! He starts singing, he lifts his arm, he talks to himself. In less than a quarter of an hour he'll be at Zamperon.

A little girl who was grazing her white nanny goat by the side of the path turned, dropped her rope and ran off screaming.

He laughed even louder than before.

"What's the matter with her? Hey, kid!"

She vanished round a bend.

The goat ran off too, leaping in bounds from ledge to ledge, trailing its rope behind it.

"You too? Hey! What's wrong? Hey, goatie!"

By now he's reached the bend himself, and three or four chalets come into view. The door of one of them is open and above the raised cap of its chimney floats a wisp of white smoke like the feathery cap of a reed.

That's what you get when you burn damp wood.

A woman comes to the door. The little girl can be heard screaming again. The woman turns towards him.

She disappears inside.

She reappears with the girl in her arms. With the corner of her apron she is covering the girl's head. Behind her is a boy of fourteen or fifteen.

The woman runs off, but the boy stays put for a moment, standing quite still in front of the door. Then he runs off too.

As for him, he says to himself, "Hello if you're here and hello if you're not." He enters the big, low room where it is dark and no light comes from the hearth because the fire has been smothered.

"This is the Donneloye house, right? Is anybody here?"

There is nobody there, but so what? He sees something good to eat hanging from a hook in the ceiling. There's butter and fresh bread on a shelf. He breaks the loaf over his knee, dips his finger in the butter. There's milk in a jug. It's a good thing they made themselves scarce. He unhooks the hunk of dried meat which is narrow and long, not much thicker than a sausage, and threaded through with a string. He sinks his teeth into it. He drinks, he eats. He eats and drinks at the same time. He chews noisily, unseeing, unhearing, oblivious to everything except the good taste and the warmth spreading through his body. The noise his mouth makes, the noise his stomach makes, after days and days on nothing but dry bread and water! How many was it? he wonders. Like being in prison, but worse, because at least in prison you can see, more or less.

He doesn't move. He's happy. He remains sitting on the bench, his elbows on the table. So good! Then he says to himself, "Now then…" He's forgotten where he is. He's forgotten where he has come from.

Ah, that's it, the mountain! The mountain? Yes, you remember. Ah! So you have to get going. "That's right," he says to himself, "It's the mountain that fell down."

And suddenly he is afraid because the mountain is still so close.

What if it fell on you again? What if it started falling again?

"Anybody there? Well, thanks anyway."

Behind him on the hearth the fire gives off a white smoke, having been smothered in wet pine needles.

Thanks very much.

He feels lightheaded. Still, he can see the path in front of him. He sees that he came from the right. So I should turn left, he tells himself.

The birds come now, more and more of them. It's as if there are two streams, one flowing beneath him and the other above.

There are woodpeckers, jays, woodpigeons, the little birds of the hedgerows, more and more of them, making more and more noise. "Yes it's me," he says, "But be quiet now."

Fatigue overtakes him, and he falls down onto the mossy verge.

III

That evening, Thérèse had gone up to a little garden that belonged to her mother, that lay just above the village, not far from the path to Derborence.

She was still alive, after all, and the baby was alive inside her. She continued to live. She had got up from her bed, she came, she went, she had even gone back to work.

There are now eight widows and thirty-five orphans in the village, and all of them are alive. That's the way it is. You split a tree down the middle, it heals. A cherry tree, if it is injured, seeps a white sap to cover its wound.

She was thin and a little haggard, is all. On the pale side, under her tan, and dressed all in black.

She bent down, she straightened up. When she lent forward, she felt the child push up against her chest. "Thank god for him," she thought. "At least he hasn't left me. At least he's faithful."

The child kept her company and the thought of him consoled her in her solitude. But then it occurred to her that he would have no father.

"What will become of us?"

She tired quickly, even though she was strong. A few strokes with the hoe and she was out of breath. There'll only be me to raise him, me on my own, me a woman...

Night was closing in. It would fall earlier than usual because of the stormy weather.

Weary, she straightened up and, resting her hands on the hoe, looked straight ahead. The sky over the high mountains had turned black where, just a moment earlier, the sun had set in a blaze of colour, as if someone had shoved a torch flames first into the sand.

A man passes by beneath her on the path, and then a woman who is in a hurry to get home. Then nobody, but the air grows darker around Thérèse, as if a pastille of colour were dissolving in water.

The bushes on the hillside seem to be melting from underneath, like butter in a pan.

It was time she went in, but she didn't have the strength. She felt unable to make a decision, unable even to move, so she stayed put, bent forward under the black sky.

And that's how she was when she thought she saw something, a pale thing that had stirred behind the bushes a short distance in front of her.

It happens, in her condition: you think you've seen something but it turns out to exist only in your head. Your thoughts get jumbled up. You have cravings, your sense of taste is altered. You can't always tell the difference between what's real and what you've imagined.

She looks again, more closely this time.

Again a white thing moves behind the bushes, fifty or so metres in front of her.

Who knows where it had sprung from. It seemed to float in the air, the lower part of it being hidden by foliage. She tried to think it through: "What could it be?" "Someone from the village," she thought, but villagers have hobnailed boots that make a noise, whereas the thing over there was silent. It slipped soundlessly from side to side. It moved, then it stopped. It was like the top part of one of those characters made out of four branches and an old smock, that they plant in gardens to scare off the sparrows. Except that this thing kept moving, making a bobbing motion every now and then. Little by little Thérèse's astonishment gave way to anxiety, and anxiety to fear, because as she watched she had the sensation that she was also being watched. The sensation grew stronger and stronger, until she let go of the handle of her hoe so that it fell among the clods of earth. She didn't call out, her voice having left her. Her heart made a noise like when you thump a door with your fist, and it doesn't open, so you thump harder. She remained there like that until a raucous croak reached her. A voice, or was it?

"Hey...! Hey...!"

A clearing of the throat that seemed, eventually, to form itself into something resembling words. She thought she heard it say, "Is that you, Thérèse?" But she heard nothing more after that, having turned tail and run.

Lightning appeared in the sky. She was lit up, she ran. She ran, she was lit up. In that instant the path appeared like a white thread weaving through the brilliant green grass, then there was no more grass and no path either.

She kept on running. Someone spoke to her: "My god, what is it?"

She sees that she has climbed the staircase. Suddenly the fire is blazing in front of her, in the kitchen hearth.

"What is it now, Thérèse?"

She dropped onto the bench without answering, pressing her hands together between her knees.

The rumble of thunder could be heard far away.

"Where's your basket? And your hoe?"

The lightning continued. There was a window in the wall of the kitchen opposite her, then there wasn't.

A window of dazzling white that formed, then unformed, then reformed. She was lit up, then not, then lit up again.

"Oh!"

You saw her, holding her head forward, then you didn't.

"He'll get wet!" she said, out of the blue. Then: "If it's him…"

She said, "Maybe it's him, maybe it's not… They can't get wet… The rain passes through them, poor things, they don't feel it…"

You saw Philomène lift her arms and then drop them again, because it was her turn to be lit up.

The whole kitchen is lit up, the whole kitchen is in darkness. The fire has time to glow red before vanishing again.

"What are you talking about?"

"Oh, you know…"

She seemed not to be aware of the storm, nor even to hear it, though it had erupted in a great downpour that rattled against the roof like the feet of dancers on a dance-floor.

"You know what they say…"

She raised her voice as the sound of the rain grew louder.

"Who?"

"The people from Zamperon, what they say about Plan, the shepherd…"

Philomène shrugged.

"He knows things, does Plan," said Thérèse. "He's old. And he says he hears them at night, because they're alive and not alive, of this earth and not of this earth."

"Well," said Philomène, "to think of all the masses we've had said… One every Sunday for your poor husband and for Séraphin."

"It may not be enough," said Thérèse, "because they're unburied… They may be trapped in purgatory at the place where they died, having died without the sacrament… So they come here to complain to us, to complain to me."

She spoke calmly. The storm had moved off, passing behind the mountain.

The downpour had given way to a fine, gentle rain. The fire glowed again, the lamp shone.

"They come out because they need us… Perhaps they see us and recognise us, even though they're nothing more than a puff of air… Perhaps one of them misses me…"

"What are you talking about?"

"Oh I don't know," she says. "I was afraid because he weighs nothing at all."

The bolts of lightning had become fewer and further between, they had changed colour. It's going away. Does everything go away? It's passing, because everything must pass. He once had a body but now no more.

"Listen," says Philomène, "should I fetch Maurice Nendaz?"

Because she too was beginning to feel frightened.

"We're two women alone here," she says. "He'll know what to do."

She blows her nose. She finds her cape and wraps it around her head and shoulders.

Thérèse has said nothing.

Philomène goes out, but she stays seated, her elbows on her knees. The rain, light now, makes a soft pattering sound like hundreds of birds' feet on the roof.

You hear nothing more. You hear the noise of a cane. You hear uneven footsteps on the staircase.

She hadn't moved.

A man spoke to her: "Come now, Thérèse…"

"Oh," she said, clutching her head in her hands, shaking it slowly, "but I saw it…"

"What did you see?"

"Him."

Maurice Nendaz said, "Where?"

"I was in the garden, it was white, there was no substance to it. You've heard the rumours, Maurice Nendaz, you know what Plan says. So what do you make of it? What if they really have come back? Only now they float above the ground, because they've got no weight. They make no noise, they're like smoke, a wisp of cloud, they go where they please…"

"We'll see about that," says Maurice Nendaz. "You said it was…"

"Right by the path," she says.

"Look here," says Maurice Nendaz, "don't get yourself in a state… It's probably your condition. Just make sure you close the house up properly… As for me, well I'll go and take a look. If I see something, I'll come and tell you. If I don't, I won't. Alright?"

"Of course," said Philomène, "you've put our minds at rest."

As for her, she said nothing, she sat there in the same position.

The sound of the cane receded into the night.

IV

He wakes towards the end of the afternoon. He has slept five hours solid.

He doesn't know where he is any more. It's Antoine.

He looks around, sees that it will soon be evening, but why he is there, all alone, deep in this gorge, he can't recall.

Sitting on the moss he begins to feel cold. The sun has left him, having passed over the tops of the mountains and gone down the other side. He feels his body all over again, his legs, his chest, and wonders, "Who's this?" He answers himself: "It's me."

Pleased, he gets to his feet.

He doesn't really know where he's going, nor where he's come from. His thoughts are mixed up, but the birds have returned, more and more of them to show him the way.

There's also the stream, which you can see if you lean over

Antoine follows the stream, follows the birds which keep coming in ever greater numbers. No longer just the great solitary birds like the eagle, that glide lugubriously over precipices in the high mountains. Not just the hawk that spies its prey from a great height, cowering among the rocks. Not even just the choughs that you see twisting and turning in the sky, black with a yellow beak, fluttering around the crevice where they've built their nest.

Smaller, tamer birds, birds of the lower places, where the rock gives way to pasture and pasture to forest: screaming jays, cooing woodpigeons, and then all the birds of the hedgerows, green, grey, brown, all one colour or with splashes of yellow, red, blue. Birds with collars, birds with dashes of colour in their tails, not counting the magpies. They rose up in front of him, more and more of them, and showed him the way.

Antoine was glad to see them, and they were glad to see him, even if a little fearful, breaking off their song, or in the case of the blackbird, shrieking in terror. "Stop!" he said to them. "Wait for me! Where are you going?" He greeted them with laughter because they heralded the lands below, they heralded warmth, home, a proper bed, bread and wine in abundance. "Hello there... Hey, wait! Don't be afraid, it's me."

He parts his hair so he can see. And suddenly he remembers something. "Ah, yes, that's right, it's me." He repeats, "The mountain fell down, but I got out."

He sets off at a run, but he has to stop again, because the shreds of his shoes have shrivelled up on drying out, and they're hurting him. He sits down, he sees that his feet are bleeding. They're grey like the earth with brown stains. He takes off his shoes, or what's left of them, and hurls them into the gorge.

Just there the gorge drops sheerly at least two hundred metres. The path is cut out of the rock that forms one wall of it.

Now he can walk more easily, though he has to watch out for sharp or pointed stones. The birds continue to flutter about in front of him, because there are bushes again here, more and more of them as you go down.

"And what's more, I have a wife."

He says to himself, "But is she waiting for me…?"

He shakes his head as he walks.

"And what about the others?"

He walks, shaking his head.

"How long since it happened?"

But he doesn't know, and he doesn't know the answers to the other questions either. He realises that he doesn't know anything. Only that he is a man called Antoine Pont, who was trapped under a rockslide, and who got out. So…

So what?

So he's heading back down.

He tries to think it through. Where is he heading down to? To his home. That is, to a house. And inside that house is a wife.

In the house I'm going to, there's a wife who is mine. But what's her name?

He understands that he has to relearn everything. He has to relearn the world, the sky, the trees, the birds. "Well at least there's one I know… The way it twitches its tail, it's easy. Hey, little bird!" He sees a dark-plumed wagtail at the end of a branch, and indeed it is wagging its tail. But the birds are beginning to roost now, because night is falling and the gorge yawns up into the darkening sky.

He hurries on as fast as he can. "It's you, you've come!" he says to the trees. "Here you are!" he says to the birds and the trees. "Me too. Me, I'm Antoine. The mountain fell down on me."

He keeps going until he reaches the place where the path leaves the gorge and the great Rhone valley opens up before your eyes.

He sees the Rhone, he says, "The mountain fell down."

Who's he talking to? The Rhone. Because the Rhone is there, in front of him. It is still light enough to make it out, white and sinuous, like a snake on stony ground, under the mountains which are becoming weighed down with clouds. He sees it well enough to recognise it. "There it is," he thinks. "So I turn left here."

He walks parallel to the river, but high up and against the current.

It is light enough, still, that he can make out the shapes of trees: low, round, apple trees, pointed pear trees, the apple trees like balls, the pear trees more elongated, taller... So it's to the left, not far now. And turning his gaze in that direction, he glimpses the village with its low stone roofs all huddled together, the village which resembles a quarry on the hillside (that is, a place where men toil to bring what's deep under the earth up above it).

He runs, he stops. He has left the path. It smells strong, warm, it smells of earth baked by the sun, of dry grass, thyme and mint, because he's walking on it, and it's soft beneath his feet. The warm stone (on this slope he's on), the ripening wheat, the promise of the grape.

He has left the path, he is cutting across bushes and pine, and it is now that he sees her, or thinks he sees her, a woman ahead of him dressed all in black. Isn't that the garden? Of course, it's our garden! She bends down, she straightens up, she stands still.

Is it her? Yes of course it's her.

He wants to call out, but his voice startles him, it is so rough, so reluctant to come forth. It is as if it had got caught on hooks in his throat, so that the words he forms never get any further.

"Hey!" he says. "Hey!"

That's all.

"Hey, woman!" he shouts.

But all of a sudden, the woman is no longer there.

"I saw nothing," said Maurice Nendaz. "Nothing at all..."

It was the next morning.

"I came up here last evening, because his poor wife thought she'd seen him."

He'd been up since dawn.

He was with Rebord and his cane. He'd been to fetch Rebord. Rebord had come down his wooden staircase.

A light rain had fallen all night, it had only just stopped. At that hour, the sky was like a dark grey slab of stone wedged halfway up the mountains.

The two men tipped their heads back pointlessly. Nendaz said, "We have to climb a little further, she insisted it was close to her garden that she saw him."

"After last night's rain?" said Rebord.

He didn't seem keen to go on. He was a fat man.

Nendaz was small and thin. Nendaz bent over his cane.

"She imagined it," said Rebord.

"Of course," said Nendaz, "she's a woman. But I promised her I'd go take a look."

As they talked, lights appeared in the windows behind them, one here, another there, a third a little farther away. They formed red pinpricks amid the crowded confusion of the houses, like the glowing embers of cigars. And at the eastern extremity of the valley, it was as if someone had inserted the tip of a crowbar between the mountains and the sky.

They were pressing down on the crowbar. The slab of fog lifted fractionally off the mountain.

They pressed, the sky lifted, it fell back down again, it lifted again. And suddenly a glorious light slipped through the opening and streamed down on top of us.

As if someone had lifted a tombstone. Life enters. Life touches that which is dead and it shudders at the contact. A horizontal beam of light, like an arm extended, points and says, "Get up!" The roofs of the village appear with their chimneys, some of which are smoking in the pale light, and meanwhile one of our cheeks is illuminated and the other is not.

Nendaz had one cheek illuminated, Rebord had one cheek illuminated.

"Get up," it said. "Leave your slumber, leave death…"

And they did. You heard it in a thousand little noises, you saw it in myriad signs, all over they were coming out of death. The lights multiplied even as they faded. Someone coughed, another blew his nose, a person called out, a door opened.

And once again, over there in the east, the crowbar went down. The fog lifted clear of the mountain and split in two, so that now the light spilled down on you not only from the side, but from directly above, and you could see one another in your entirety, put back together, set upright again.

"Well!" said Rebord. "Can you see anything?"

"Not a thing!" said Nendaz.

And yet, from where they stood, they commanded the hillside and the path that led to Derborence. In front of them, in an arc, lay the gardens: two or three of them. Beyond these the slope became steeper, climbing straight up to the sky, and in the rock, the pines, the bushes it recovered its former colours – grey, russet, blackish with green stripes.

"So?" said Rebord.

"So what?" said Nendaz.

"We should turn back," said Rebord. He still wasn't convinced, and since Nendaz stayed put, scanning the hillside, he added, "It's the old man's fault... Yes, old Plan, the shepherd. He's bewitched that lot from Zamperon. As if the rest of us hadn't done our best. Prayers, masses... The least they could do is keep quiet, don't you think?"

Nendaz simply nodded.

In front of them stood a little hayloft that had been built at the border of the fields and the trees. It belonged to a man named Dionis Udry who just then emerged from his house and set off towards it. It was a hundred metres away at most. They saw Dionis open the door of the loft, which wasn't locked. He pulled it towards him, but instead of going inside, they saw him take a step backwards. Then, tipping his head to one side, he thrust it into the gap.

Suddenly he turned towards Nendaz whom he must have noticed in passing. He waved, beckoning him closer.

Nendaz put his foot and his cane forward at the same time.

"You're going?" said Rebord.

"Of course."

Nendaz went. Rebord hesitated, then decided to follow him, but at a distance: two metres, then three metres. Dionis hadn't moved, and as Nendaz came up to him, he said, "Come and see this... Someone slept here last night, come quickly and see... I haven't touched anything."

Nendaz peers inside. The loft is three quarters full. The hay forms a slope that rises up from the door to the roof on the opposite side. On that slope, standing out against the mass of lightly tossed chaos, is a smooth place, a place where the hay is like felt, like clay, a place where a body had moulded itself.

"What is it?" says Dionis.

Nendaz scratches the back of his ear.

"Don't know."

"But someone was here?"

"Oh yes."

"Who could have come through here?"

Suddenly Rebord breaks in: "Good god, you can't be too careful… I'm going to get my gun."

It was he who sowed panic in the village, because he said to the people he passed, "Watch out, there's a thief about."

He had made up his mind. He climbed his staircase and reappeared with an old flintlock pistol, a powder flask, a bag of bullets.

The villagers watched him load his gun, pouring in the powder and tamping it down, pushing the ramrod up and down the barrel, sitting on one of his steps, while his wife stood on the top step and lent over him.

"Don't go! Rebord, stay here. D'you hear? Don't go!"

The neighbours looked on, bemused.

The sun was fully up. It promised to be a beautiful day. The sky had crazed over like dry earth as it had risen, sliding up the flanks of the mountains. You could see a long way in front of you and a long way above you, the air being as pure and clean as a newly washed window. The last of the night's rain, lingering in round drops on the leaves, added a thousand tiny fires in all the colours of the rainbow. A cock crowed again, with gusto, its beak open wide. And as if summoned by that sound, he appeared up above. Nendaz saw him first, then Dionis, but neither knew what he was looking at.

It was three or four hundred metres away from them, and it was white.

It came out from behind a bush in the direction of Thérèse's garden. It appeared, then disappeared, then reappeared. It was as if someone were trying to hide themselves and see at the same time. The white thing disappeared.

But now here it was again, closer.

Dionis retreated, as if the closer the thing came, the less sure he felt. Dionis retreats,

Nendaz retreats. The sun shines down on the mountain, the sun goes in, hiding itself in its turn. The whole village has come out, forming a line at the boundary of the houses. They're all there, watching, seeing nothing, seeing something or thinking they've seen something, and in the meantime Nendaz and Dionis have joined them.

"See him?"

"No."

"There."

"Where? Can't see a thing."

Another voice: "He's over there now... behind the burnt pine."

"One thing's for sure," says Dionis, "someone slept in my loft last night..."

Then a woman cries out, "I know, I know who it is!"

"Who?" they ask her.

"The dead... They've come back, you can't stop them."

Someone leads her away.

But now the idea spreads quickly between them, it enters their minds and fear enters with it. Because if it is the dead, she's right, how can we stop them coming? How can we stop them entering our houses, they who recognise neither doors nor locks?

One man took up a pitchfork, another a big stick, a third armed himself with his flail. There weren't many men, because of those who had died and those who were away in the mountain huts. It was a summer village, a village of women, children and a few old people.

They saw nothing for a moment, then suddenly the white dot appeared heading straight down towards them. It had been hidden for a moment, having traversed a copse.

Several women ran away, others stopped at the bottom of their steps or in front of their doors, so as to be able to take shelter if need be.

A gun went off.

It was Rebord shooting into the air. The white spot vanished.

They threw themselves on Rebord. They said to him, "What are you doing? You're crazy! We don't even know who it is, or what it is. You could do some serious damage."

He shook his head: "I shot in the air."

RBORENCE

He said, "It's my business."

He reloaded his gun, they couldn't stop him, and tipping his head back, he said, "See, it's gone."

He pointed at the hillside.

"There's nobody there."

Maurice Nendaz (who was a thoughtful man) beckoned to Justin. He took him aside and whispered to him.

Justin ran off towards Premier, where the parish church was.

Meanwhile the others were busy gesticulating, meanwhile the women led the children away who had been terrified by the gunshot, meanwhile they pointed to the hillside where nothing now moved, where no living thing stirred. But is living the right word? Should we really say living? Do we know what it's made of? Does it weigh anything? Perhaps it's nothing more than air. Perhaps it's a shape that exists only for the eyes, that is, then isn't, that appears, then disappears. Then a woman's voice was heard.

"Where is he?"

And again: "Who let off the gun? You frightened him... Now he'll never come back!"

It was Thérèse.

"It's him, I know it's him. Last night, in the dark, I wasn't sure, but if you saw him in broad daylight... Where is he?"

Nendaz took one of her arms, Dionis the other.

"Where is he? I want to go and get him."

Philomène was there too, standing behind her daughter. There was a man to the right of Thérèse, a man to the left of her, but she stood out a little ahead of them all. She said, "Let go of me!"

They spoke to her.

"No, stay here, we don't know yet. And see," said Nendaz, "there's nothing there any more, he's gone."

She stopped moving, she seemed to become docile. Everyone looked, but there was nothing to see.

Suddenly a small, pale sun illuminated the hillside in a palette of pleasing colours, turning the trunks of the pines red, causing certain rocks to dazzle like window-panes. He was hiding.

Someone said, "Oh!"

With an abrupt movement of her shoulders Thérèse had freed herself. She set off at a run, straight ahead. Nendaz ran after her, but he couldn't catch her because of his bad leg. She ran to the end of the gardens, to the bottom of the stony slope, and there she stopped.

"Antoine! Antoine! It's me..."

She said, "Antoine! Is it you...?"

And those watching saw the white spot reappear high up, three hundred metres from her, rising from behind a bush where he must have hidden himself the moment the gun went off.

Someone with the body of a man, but who no longer looks like a man, as she sees better now, from where she is; who watches her, who hesitates.

She hesitates too. She tries to recognise him, she fails. It's clearly a man or something like a man, with a beard but no eyes. He has a mouth, but is there a tongue in his mouth? Something black hangs down over the top of his face. He's almost naked with a body the colour of stone, a body that resembles a corpse... She backs up a bit.

He stays put.

Seeing her retreat, Nendaz comes up to her with his cane.

"Wait, Thérèse, wait... We don't know yet, we'll know better soon."

But the chapel bell has begun to ring.

A shepherd was caught under the rockfall at Derborence. He was trapped under the debris for close to two months. He reappeared; nobody could believe it. It was at that moment that the chapel bell rang out, because there's only one chapel hereabouts, and the priest from Premier comes to it once a week to say mass. A tiny little bell, with a voice as clear as a child's. It came, it was heard, it grew and rippled outwards on the air; then, as when a wave strikes the shore and retreats, it collided with the hillside which sent it back.

It came back. It circled above us like a sparrowhawk, the one hunters call "the good bird".

Now the priest from Premier, whom Justin had gone to fetch, appeared among the houses.

He is black and white. In front of him he carries the monstrance, which glints. A choirboy who is red and white carries the cross.

He passes close to the fountain, we kneel. We are no longer afraid. He advances, he is behind the cross; the cross goes in front.

He comes near to where Thérèse is. Thérèse kneels. She lowers her head, then raises it again, still on her knees, and looks in the direction that the cross and the monstrance are moving. We'll soon find out if it's really him. If it's him or the shadow of him. If he is flesh or ghost. If he exists in reality or merely in illusion. Meanwhile the Our Father and the cross reach the place where the slope turns steep.

She clasps her hands together.

As for him…

He takes a step forwards, he stops. He has come out from behind his bush, he takes another step forward, then one to the side, like a drunkard. Then he stops.

Are you a man? Are you Christian? Are you of this world? He wants to reply, we see that. But he can't, he is not yet able. He takes a step, he stands still, he takes another step.

Is it you, Antoine Pont?

Come, because we will wait, if it is you. Our Lord awaits you, along with the instrument of his suffering. Two hands hold the wooden cross aloft before you. Is it really you, Antoine Pont, husband of Thérèse Maye, Christian and son of a Christian?

The bell keeps ringing.

The man comes forward again, this time he doesn't stop, he comes faster and faster. Is it him? Yes it's him, because he comes right up to the cross. And the cross gleams in the sunlight that is breaking over the mountains.

The bell is still ringing.

He stoops, he bows his head and neck. Then, throwing himself forward, he falls onto his knees.

V

She looked at him from a distance, she said, "Is it really you, Antoine?"

He looked at her.

"And you, is it really you?"

Laughing, he turned his back on her. She had expected him to dance for joy. She had expected him to come to her, take her face in his hands and never let her go. Oh! The things they would tell each other, so many things. They would be standing up or sitting down. Or perhaps they would begin by standing up and then he would say, "Sit." And they would talk for hours, softly, each aware of the warmth of the other's body, and then they would stop talking, because there would be nothing more to say.

But there it is, he burst out laughing.

The kitchen was still full of steam and the smell of soap. He had washed himself. They'd brought him clothes and underwear. Rebord, who as well as selling drink had a second line as a barber, had cut his hair and shaved him carefully.

Antoine looked at himself in the mirror: "How thin my face is!"

He looked again.

"No bigger than a fist... And unhealthy looking. It's hardly surprising, after two months underground... And then that Rebord goes and shoots at me! Well he was a soldier once."

"Antoine!"

But he went on: "That there is a book... Is it your missal?"

She was watching him closely, albeit from afar, as if she didn't dare come closer.

"Is it really you, Antoine?"

"Touch me, I'm flesh and bone, the cross never lies. Touch me and see if you're dreaming. I'm solid, I won't go up in smoke, it's me alright."

"Is it possible?"

"Now that over there..."

And he carried on making an inventory of all the objects in the bedroom. He moved around the room, naming them one by one.

"Ah!" he said. "That's the brooch I gave you."

A crowd had gathered in front of the house, but nobody dared enter. Old Philomène was tidying the kitchen. She went out with a pail of soapy water and emptied it at the base of the wall.

"Well? Is it him?" they asked her. "How is he?"

Just then he opened a window beneath which a group of children had gathered. He pushed his white face towards them and howled, frightening them. They scattered in all directions, like a murmuration of starlings in the vines when a gun goes off.

He brought his head and torso back into the bedroom, laughing. And straight away he resumed his inspection of the walls because, as he said, "I have to relearn everything."

She would have liked to go to him, to take him in her arms and hold him tight; she didn't dare.

She had many things to tell him, she found nothing to say. Astonishment had chased them out of her mind.

She would have liked to say, "Listen, I have a surprise for you, a nice surprise." But he said, "Look, a chair…! That's for sitting on."

He sat, laughing. Why was he laughing? He laughed, and then he went back to his inventory.

"Look at that, a pin cushion! So you still sew?"

"What month are we in?" he asked suddenly. "And the day? And the date?"

"I've lived seven weeks fewer than you, than all of you. Now that I'm back in time, I have to catch up."

There was a knock at the kitchen door. It was the mayor.

"Can Antoine come? The priest wants to speak to him."

He was ready. He had only to put on his hat. The crowd waited in the street and down the side of the house. He opened the door. They looked at him in amazement, barely recognising him. "He's a lot thinner than he was," they said. "Is it him? Is it really him? Why, he's nothing but skin and bone!"

And yet they pushed forward to shake his hand, women, men, neighbours, children too, though they were timid and in awe. He said nothing, he simply laughed. The mayor walked beside him. It was a beautiful day and a cool breeze blew, freshening one cheek.

He walked beside the mayor, the others being forced to follow because of the narrowness of the street. He was a little unsteady on his legs. They marvelled to see him in daylight, he seemed such a stranger to the sun. His complexion was that of a plant that pushes up from under dead leaves, or of a vegetable that's been stored in the cellar to whiten. He turned to the crowd and laughed. "I'm not myself, see," he said to the mayor. "I was under the stones…"

"It'll be alright," the mayor replied. "We're here."

"But I'm not under the stones any more…" Antoine went on, and he breathed in deeply, hungrily. "Oh it's good!" He turned round, he said, "It's good, but it makes my head spin."

He spent nearly an hour shut up with the priest and the mayor.

Now the crowd was gathered in front of the village hall. The news had spread fast and some had come from Premier, meaning that there were more trousers than usual, among the skirts. "What's he doing?" they asked. "They're questioning him," came the reply.

Finally he emerged. "I have to get back to my wife," he said. "I've barely seen her."

"What about us?" they cried. "She'll have all the time in the world to see you, later. We're just passing through."

It was the men from Premier who were blocking his path.

"Greetings!" they said. "Is it you? If it is you, you're half the size you were."

Seeing Antoine so close, some turned away in fear, or went to hide behind others, and from that vantage point they observed him: his face, his hands, his legs, what was left of his body beneath his baggy clothes (which did indeed make him look like a scarecrow). They saw from afar the hollows beneath his cheekbones, his cracked lips, his yellow teeth that stuck out – a dead man among the living.

"Impossible!"

They needed proof, and not just that which their eyes could furnish, but also that which came courtesy of their ears and hands. They needed to hear him speak, to run their hands over his clothes.

"Come!" they said.

Rebord took one arm, Dionis took the other, and they escorted him to Rebord's place. "We'll have a drink," they said.

They helped him up the stairs, making a great noise as they did so. The staircase complained, you could feel it sagging under the weight, would it hold? They all got in, at least as many as could squeeze into the saloon. Others stood about beneath the windows or went to drink in nearby houses.

They sat him down at the table at the end of the room, so that he faced the light. "Are you hungry?" they asked.

"Bring him some cheese and some dried meat," they said to Rebord. "You owe him that at least…"

They said, "Where's your gun, you crazy old man? Hidden it well away, have you? You'd better not pull another stunt like that…"

To Antoine they said, "Your health!"

They put down their glasses and looked at him. People kept coming, climbing the staircase, staring at him through the open window before they ventured in.

They said nothing. A few went noiselessly back down the steps, but others couldn't contain themselves.

"Pont!"

Raising his head, he turned on them a pair of troubled eyes, eyes that seemed hurt by the light.

"It's you, Pont! Unbelievable… Where did you come from? How did you get out from under?"

The village buzzed like a disturbed beehive.

VI

"Wait!" he said. "Let me get my thoughts in order. Where am I? Oh yes! I got out from under the earth, and now here you are, and here I am, and here we are!"

"Your health!"

"It's funny, though, because they questioned me at the village hall, and now I don't know any more. It comes and goes…"

"Your health, Antoine!"

"But if you're finishing up the harvest, then explain to me, because you hadn't got going with the hay when… No, you hadn't started yet. Ah, I remember! What day is it? What's the date? I've already asked my wife that. What did you say? Really? The seventeenth of August? The seventeenth of August in which year? Because for a long time I lived outside years, you see, outside weeks and days…"

They answered his questions.

"You have to count, I can't do it. You count," he said to Nendaz. "How many does that make?"

"It makes seven weeks and maybe a little more. Nearly eight weeks."

"Unbelievable!"

Sat at his table, surrounded by people, a glass in front of him.

"You get out of the habit of day, see, because you only catch a glimpse of it from time to time, somewhere above you. It's there, and then it's not there. Way up above, in the gaps between the stones… Because the mountain fell down."

Air entered. Wasps, bees came in; flies. Every kind of fly, blue ones, green ones, black ones that formed a kind of fog around you. The black ones clustered around your head like one of those muslins you swathe yourself in before you reach into the hive to get the honey. He was inside it; he brought his pale, sunken eyes to rest on you without actually seeing you.

People came in, people went out. "Keep it down!" they told each other. Oblivious, his gaze turned inwards, he continued to follow the things that filed through the space behind his eyes, that is to say one thing, and then another thing.

"Wait, it's coming back to me… The mountain fell down…"

He asked, "Did you hear it from here, when the mountain fell down?"

"We certainly did," said Nendaz, "but we didn't know what it was. We thought it was a storm, but it was a clear night."

"Really, a clear night?"

"And how! Stars like you've never seen and not a cloud in the sky. So everyone went back to bed... Everyone except me. Ask Justin. Because I had an idea that maybe it was something else after all."

"I didn't hear anything," said Antoine. "It wasn't noise, it was too big for the ears. It was as if a knee were pressing down on me, and I came tumbling down from the wall with the plank and the mattress. The plank, the mattress and me, there we were, all three of us, on the floor..."

"Listen," they said. "Listen. Be quiet, you!"

The one with the broken arm had turned up.

"I had a beam come crashing down on my shoulder," he said. "They set it for me with splints."

But Antoine went on as if there had been no interruption.

"The mountain fell down, see, the mountain fell on top of me, so I lay still on the floor, because I didn't know if I'd be able to move and anyway I couldn't be bothered. How long did I stay like that? Who knows? And then there was this person..."

It was as if he had actually caught sight of the person, somewhere inside himself.

"This person called out to me... Yes..."

But he seemed to have forgotten the person he was talking about, so we didn't find out who it was. He had already moved on.

"I was concentrating on not moving, not going to see what had happened, wondering if I was still in one piece. Because my spine could easily have been snapped in two, see? And then he said, 'Where are you?' And I replied, 'Here.' And that was that. I tried moving my right hand, just the fingertips to begin with, then the hand, then the arm as far as the elbow, then the whole arm..."

"Greetings Antoine!" someone said.

Two men from Premier had come in. He went on: "I thought, 'One works, now let's try the other.' And with my right arm I examined the left."

"Aren't you drinking?" they asked him.

"I'm drinking," he said, "thanks. So I lifted up the left arm..."

He laughed, and those around him laughed too.

"But there were still the two legs, and at the same time I'm thinking, 'Did someone call me?' Nobody was calling me any more, at any rate. I caught sight of one of my knees, then the other, and that makes two. I tried waggling them, like a baby when you undress it, and both seemed to work."

We spoke to him, we asked him questions, but he wasn't listening. He was following his memories as they came back to him, but they were coming in no particular order. They yanked him forward, they dragged him back.

"Finally I sat up and saw that nothing was missing, that I had two arms, two legs and a body, not counting the head. And when I lifted my arm... because I could lift it, see... So I lifted it, and three inches above my head I found a sort of ceiling. Because the mountain had fallen down, and a big crumb of it was slanting down over me. I was in the angle, stuck beneath it. I was buried alive, so to speak. The twenty-third of June, you say? Yes, the twenty-third of June, around two in the morning, it must have been. And I started yelling, yelling with all my strength, as if anyone could have heard me..."

He picked up his glass. And now it was his turn to say, "Your health! And to you, Placide, your very good health. So you're here, are you? And you broke your arm? What about the others?"

Nobody answered him, but he had already forgotten his own question.

"Because you see, you're stupid at moments like that. I shouted as loud as I could, then I thought to myself, 'Better save air,' and I stopped shouting. It occurred to me that I might not have air for very long, so I tried to breathe as little as I could. I closed my mouth, I pressed my lips together and I breathed through my nose, in little sniffs, like this..."

He pinched his nose to demonstrate.

"Because imagine if I'd been short of air, not just space and light, but air too..."

"What about bread?" they said.

"Wait."

"And water?"

"Don't be in such a hurry," he told them. "What use is any of that, without air? Air comes before bread or water. And I was happy to see that at least I didn't have to worry about air, because it came through the gaps in the rocks, which were piled up on top of each other. There was this great thick layer of rock, but it was full of cracks and the air found its way through them. So I got onto my hands and knees, since it wasn't possible to stand, and that's when I saw how lucky I'd been, because the whole back part of the chalet, where it meets the rock, was intact…"

He went on: "We had made two cheeses, already, and we'd brought up enough bread to last us six weeks. Well as luck would have it, the bread and the cheese had ended up on the right side of things, that is to say, on a shelf against the rock, so that by following the rockface with my hand…"

"Ah!" they said. And Antoine: "See? And I still had the mattress too…"

They saw. He went on.

You have to imagine that the bulk of the landslide was pierced through with tunnels that went in all directions, as in a sponge. Unfortunately, these tunnels didn't link up. One stopped here, another opened up just beside it, but between the end of one and the beginning of the other there was no way through; hopeless. The blockage might not be very thick, but it was as unforgiving as a wall, being made of stone: solid, smooth, compact stone. Only dynamite could have shifted it. And now, perhaps, you can begin to understand why he lost so much time. Seven whole weeks… count them!

He would wriggle along a tunnel on his belly for as long as he could, then turn into another tunnel, still on his belly, and then he'd be on his knees and he'd notice that the rock beneath him was following an upward incline… He was still talking: "I'd get excited when it climbed, because the day was above me, but then it started to slope downwards again, and I'd get disheartened."

"It took time," he said. "A day, two days, maybe three or even four. How was I to know? And you've guessed it, right? Because I had nothing to drink… My lips dried up and started to crack, my tongue felt like a piece of old leather, and my mouth grew too big for it because the roof had shrivelled up too. Each time I'd come back and lie down on my mattress, thinking, 'Rest a little.' If only I'd had a pot to piss in. You've heard the stories of travellers lost in the desert who survived by drinking their own urine…? Ah, if only you knew how lucky you were, you who live under the sky and have clocks! 'With their fountains,' I said to myself, 'Their beautiful fountains! All those springs on the surface of the earth, and nothing but a tiny bead of water that reaches me from time to time, seeping through a patch of moss…'"

Tick.

What's that sound?

They're at Rebord's, the saloon is full. He raises a finger: "Tock…"

Like a pendulum swinging, slowly at first, then faster and faster: "Tick… tock… tick… tock…"

He got up from the mattress, he felt his way with his hands, and suddenly he raised his head. Water streamed down his face, he had only to open his mouth.

"It was the meltwater that had at first been dammed, and was now winding its way down through the rocks, sending one tiny offshoot my way. It was like a cord strung taut between the roof and the ground, that I could feel moving between my hands. When I lifted my hands up I felt it wriggle inside them like a living thing. It was alive and I would live by it. So I quickly found a pail to put beneath it, thinking, 'If it ever dried up…' And that was it! I was saved. Because at that point I had everything, you see, everything we need to stay alive. I had food, water, air and something to sleep on, and now all I had to do was make use of the time of which I had plenty too. Oh, where time was concerned, as you saw, I had exactly as much as I needed. Seven weeks, more than seven weeks…"

The afternoon wore on at Rebord's.

He was interrupted from time to time by people coming in or asking questions, or because someone raised a glass to his health, and he'd be obliged to respond.

Each time he returned to his telling.

"They were like the gullies that run along beneath the mountain paths. They were so narrow I could only slip through by hugging the walls. In places where the light filtered through, I left marks so that I would be able to find my way back. Where there was no light, I went backwards and forwards until I'd learned that stretch by heart… I'd go a long way in one direction, only to find it blocked and have to come back… Sometimes, a feeble sort of light would filter down from above, and I'd try to climb up towards it, like a chimneysweep. I'd climb and climb, and suddenly I'd be confronted by a spur of rock sticking out into the shaft, and be forced to go back down again. Then daylight would appear to my left, and off I'd go chasing it like a new shoot. A shoot is spindlier than thread and stronger than an iron bar, but I had neither its strength nor its stamina, because I was constantly being lured in all directions by hopes that turned out to be false. Seven weeks," he said, "and I had to persevere and I had to be patient, because often the fault was clogged with debris, and working slowly, using only the tips of my fingers, I cleared it. Now, perhaps, you understand why it took me so long."

"Seven weeks!" he repeated.

Evening was beginning to fall.

"But you got there in the end," they said, "because here you are." And they looked at him expectantly.

"And your health is returning, that's obvious. You're already looking better."

They observed him where he sat, facing the window and the evening light. They saw the pink spots high on his cheeks.

"It's the wine, you drank too much water! Hey, Rebord, another glass over here... Yes, there, where the bone sticks out beneath the eye socket. Your health! Your very good health!"

This time, however, he didn't drink. They saw that he was lost in thought, his hand cupping his glass which rested on the table.

"How many were we?" he asked suddenly.

"Where?"

"Up there."

There was silence, then someone said, "Let's see, around twenty...?"

"Eighteen," a voice corrected.

"And how many came back?" asked Antoine.

You could hear the birds roosting in the trees. Finally someone answered him.

"Well, there's you."

Someone else said, "And Barthelémy."

"What about him?" asked Antoine. "Where is he?"

"Listen," said Nendaz, "you're tired... Let's talk about this another time."

"Where is he?" Antoine insisted.

"Well now," said Nendaz, "he was unlucky, see. He got caught under a rock."

"And?" said Antoine.

"And?" said Nendaz. "Well, yes..."

"Oh!" said Antoine. "I see. I was there, I know what it's like. That comes down on you and everything is swept away. I get it: the others, all of them, Jean-Baptiste and his son, the two Mayes, all the Carrupts, Defayes, Bruchez... I understand, but..."

He slammed his fist down on the table.

"But there's one who isn't dead... Ah, I'd forgotten! But he's alive, I tell you. It was when the mountain came down... It's my fault," he said, "it slipped my mind!"

He paused, then: "Séraphin."

Once again you heard the sound of birds roosting.

Antoine sees him. Antoine doesn't say another word, because he sees him. Antoine stares fixedly ahead. What he sees is a man who is already old and wrinkled, a man with small, light-coloured eyes embedded in orbits that lack brows. They are sitting together in front of the fire, it's around nine in the evening. Then...

Antoine brings his fist down on the table.

"He's alive, I'm telling you! I know he's alive, because he called out to me. I was on the floor with the mattress. He's a friend of mine, see. He's more than a friend, in fact, he's a father."

Those gathered round him said nothing.

"Without him, I'd never have got married, I couldn't have. He's alive! He called out to me, I was on the floor. He said, 'Hey, Antoine!' I wanted to reply, but I couldn't. 'Hey Antoine, are you there?' I wanted to say yes, but no words came. I must have passed out. But he's up there, he's alive... Séraphin!"

They still said nothing, so he spoke again. "All we have to do is find him."

All day long Thérèse's house was busy with women. They kept knocking, coming in search of news, or else it was the men calling in the hope of finding Antoine at home.

"He's not here," she had to tell them. "He went to the village hall with the mayor and the priest."

And then, as the afternoon wore on: "No, he isn't back yet. I think you'll find him at Rebord's. He went drinking with his friends..."

It's funny, because I'm his wife.

As for Philomène, she sat in front of the fire. Philomène shook her head. "It's a miracle," she said.

"Lucky indeed," people said, "to get your son-in-law and your husband back like that, after seven weeks!"

"Oh yes," said Philomène, "it's a miracle. But it's a tragedy, too, because he wasn't alone up there, though he was alone when he came back. There were two of them. My poor brother!"

She crossed herself.

"My poor brother! He died a second time…"

It was eight in the evening. Little by little the house emptied. Finally Philomène went home too, but he still wasn't back. Had he forgotten his wife? Had he forgotten that he was married? "He hasn't noticed," she said to herself, "even though it's been nearly three months…"

She stood in front of the mirror, sideways on, so that the front of her body was lit by the lamp. And studying her profile, she said, "Yes, look, it's obvious, especially when I put on my new dress, which is tighter around the waist… But he hasn't noticed a thing."

She waited a little longer in the bedroom, where the bed was turned down and the lamp cast a soft light. Meanwhile, downstairs, the evening meal was laid out on the kitchen table. Still he didn't come.

"I'll go and fetch him."

She got as far as the door and opened it. She saw that the stars were already out. But she didn't dare go any further, because of what people would say.

They would laugh at her. Running after your husband already? Leave him in peace. He wants to be with his friends, it's natural. Let them drink a glass or two together. He'll come eventually.

That's what they'd say, and they'd be right, wouldn't they? "Well then," she thought, "let him come when he wants. I'll be here. I'll sit in the kitchen so that he sees me as soon as he comes in, so that the first thing he sees is his faithful wife."

She sat very still, her hands resting in her lap.

She heard voices in the distance. They reached her quite distinctly because the village lay in silence. It was men, several men, many men.

The voices came closer.

"We'll let you go now," she heard.

Then came Nendaz's voice: "Good night, Antoine."

A third voice said, "See you soon, OK?"

Then: "Good night… Watch the step… Alright? Good night then…"

Footsteps approached. They climbed the stairs, striking each step. They stopped for a moment in front of the door. A hand sought and failed to find the latch.

She got to her feet, wanting to be there when he came in, wanting to be the first thing he saw.

"You!" he said. "So it's true… idiot! I have a wife."

He passed a hand over his face. "And that's not all."

"Antoine!" she said.

"You're called Thérèse. See, I remember… And of course we're married now, only before… we had to…"

"Antoine!" she said. "Antoine!"

"Where are my workclothes? He's alive, you see. They wouldn't believe me at Rebord's… I have to go and find him."

He walked into the room, looked around, stopped. He was like a plant that had been pulled up by its roots, a tree sawn through at its base. He had to steady himself against the doorpost before entering the bedroom.

"He's not dead, I told them. He's not dead, because he called to me. He can't get out, is all. He's trapped under the rocks."

There was nothing she could say. The lamp cast a soft light over the large bed with its sheet turned back. But he "Are they in the wardrobe?"

"Antoine! Listen, Antoine, I have something to tell you."

But he had toppled over on his side like a man who received a blow to the head. He had fallen so that the top part of his body lay face down on the sheet, while his legs trailed on the floor.

He had fallen asleep in an instant, and she saw that nothing would wake him, because she was able to remove his shoes and jacket, turn him on his back and lift up his legs. Oblivious, he put up no resistance. He was as supple and as docile as a corpse that's still warm.

He slept with his arms outstretched and his mouth open. From his mouth, at regular intervals, came a noise as loud and as grating as the rasp of a plane, such that Thérèse couldn't bring herself to do her conjugal duty and lie down beside him. She spent the night at her mother's.

And so it was that, the next morning, the neighbours saw her returning home.

"You, up and about already?" they said.

They were amazed to discover that she hadn't spent the night with her husband, but since the deed was done, they told her, "You've come too early! Let him sleep. These men, when they're worn out, they can sleep for three days. Three days and three nights solid."

And yet it was late. It was coming up to nine. When they saw Thérèse hesitate, the women said to her, "Go on then! Either he's asleep and you won't disturb him, or he's awake and he'll be glad to see you…"

They laughed. They were still laughing when she went in. She vanished, then she reappeared.

"My god! My god!"

"What is it?"

"Did you see him?"

"Who?"

"Antoine!"

"No."

"Heaven help me, he's not there!"

"Is that all?" they said. "You gave us a fright. So he's gone out, all you have to do is find him. He's got to be in the village somewhere."

But she shook her head, she kept shaking it.

"No," she said, "I know him. He's gone back."

"Gone back where?"

"Up there."

Just then a magistrate and a policeman arrived, having come up from the valley to take Antoine's statement. They had asked directions to his house, and the neighbours had pointed it out. As they approached they saw a woman at the top of the stairs making agitated gestures with her head and waving her arms in the air. Catching sight of them in turn, she gave a hollow laugh.

"You, of course you would turn up now. Perfect timing!"

Then, changing her tone, she said to them, "Oh please, go after him! Go quickly! If he's up there... Oh please, anything could happen!"

That was indeed where he had gone, having left before dawn, in his madness, and retraced his steps. Dressed in a clean white shirt and a new suit, he turned up at Biollaz's house, just before the first of the rocks that the moss has since painted gold, pale yellow, shades of grey or dark green. Just before the biggest of the blocks, the ones the size of houses, in whose cracks grew every kind of plant: bilberry, blackberry, the barberry bush with its woody fruit and tough leaves.

He put his head around the door: "Anyone there?"

And then: "Don't you recognise me?"

"Heavens no!" said Biollaz.

"Antoine."

"Antoine who? We're not short of Antoines round here."

"Antoine... Look closer... Antoine Pont, from Aïre."

"No!" Biollaz shrank back.

And then, keeping his eyes fixed on the face that he could now see in its entirety, because Antoine had removed his hat, he pictured it as it once was. He filled it out, coloured it in.

"Wait! Yes... It's you alright. But where have you sprung from?"

"From beneath the rocks," said Antoine.

He pointed to the place, not far from there.

"I was caught like the others, but I got out."

"Unbelievable!" said Biollaz. "How?"

"On my stomach, on my hands and knees... Seven weeks..."

"And where have you come from just now?"

"From the village."

"Loutre!" Biollaz called. "Hey, Loutre!"

Loutre was working nearby. He came.

"Do you know who this is?"

Loutre kept his distance. He was wary.

"No."

"And yet you know him. You've seen his initials… A.P."

"Good heavens," said Loutre, "he's scrawny enough."

"Plump him up."

"He could do with some stuffing in his cheeks."

"Stuff 'em."

"Pont!"

"That's it, Loutre. See, you can come closer, there's nothing to be afraid of."

Loutre came closer. Loutre asked in his turn, "Where have you sprung from?"

Once again Antoine pointed towards the north, in the direction of the bowl of rock and the place where the landslide had begun. Then he went on with his story, Biollaz having asked him, "When?"

"Yesterday. No, the day before."

Biollaz called again. "Hey, Marie!"

Marie was the Donneloye woman, who lived in one of the neighbouring chalets. She appeared in her doorway. Biollaz shouted to her, "Hey, Marie, remember the day before yesterday? The ghost? That's it, when you ran away. Remember he had a good appetite, and quite a nerve too? Well here he is, your ghost!"

"Ah!" she said. "Who?"

"Pont, Antoine."

Dsozet appeared beside her, poking his head forward to get a better look.

"It's true," said Antoine, "but I was hungry. Seven weeks, don't forget! True, I probably wasn't the most beautiful sight to behold… But it's me, I promise. It's me, he said to the Donneloye woman, and I'll pay you whatever I owe you, of course."

She took a few steps forward.

"So I went down to the village and eventually they realised who I was, because at the beginning they were like you… They even tried to shoot me. They took me for a ghost… We drank together," said Antoine… "They brought the priest, and then we drank together."

Dsozet had come closer too.

"The trouble is," he went on, "one of us is still up there. That's why I'm going back. You haven't seen anyone, have you? I was up before dawn, because otherwise they would have tried to stop me leaving. They would have said there was nobody to find. Well I know there is."

By now several men were gathered around Antoine, not really understanding what he was saying.

"Because he isn't dead. Séraphin, you remember him... Séraphin, Séraphin Carrupt. Quite old... Yes, that's him. The brother of my mother-in-law, and if I was finally able to tie the knot it was thanks to him, because my mother-in-law didn't want me for a son-in-law. An old friend, you see, more than a friend... And he's still there..."

"Where?"

"Up there. We were together in the chalet when the mountain fell down. Oh, I remember it well! We were sitting in front of the fire, and he asked me if I was bored. He said to me, 'Don't I count?' Much more than a friend, a father, because I'm an orphan. Well I managed to get out, but he's still up there, yes, under the rocks. I told them in the village, but they didn't believe me. That's why I've come back. I'm alone, but you'll help me. How many are you? Ten, at least. He's alive, I tell you. I remember it clearly, I was on the floor and he spoke to me. He said, 'Where are you, Antoine?' It's just that he wasn't able to find his way out."

"You think? You really think, after all this time?"

"I spent seven weeks under there. We're talking less than two days more for him. So, will you come? Of course you will. We'll try calling him. Or else we'll take a gun and fire it so that he can make his way towards the noise."

He was talking faster and faster, not making much sense, asking questions without waiting to hear the answers. The others stood around him shaking their heads, but in the end two of them went with him: Biollaz and Loutre.

The three men headed for the righthand side of the scree, aiming to get above it as quickly as possible. They climbed the steep slope and the rockfall fell away beneath them as if they were lowering it on a rope. Having appeared to bulge it now looked flat. The great blocks turned to gravel, the smaller ones to sand.

At first, when they looked up at its highest point, they saw a ridge in the form of a wave. The slope behind the ridge was hidden from view. But then they saw it, gradually the slope revealed itself, and as it did so it hollowed out; what had appeared to be a slope wasn't one after all. "Oh!" said Antoine. "Yes," said the men, "and you should have seen how it smoked!" "Smoked?" "Good God, the dust! For three days we couldn't see a thing."

Now, though, everything was visible. They could see it all, better and better, and they could hear it too. Only when the men's hobnailed boots bit the rock, making a noise like a dog crunching on a bone, was the silence disturbed. But then it was disturbed no longer, because they had reached a sort of platform where they paused while Antoine gazed at the scene beneath him. He shook his head: "To think that I got out alive!"

Then: "Well if I did, so can he."

He contemplated the disaster, that sea stopped in its tracks, all that dead vastness in which no life remained, and he said, "He's there."

Everything is dead, yet Antoine says, "He's alive." They looked closely. Nothing moved in any of those spaces, neither on the gleaming surface, nor in the holes that showed up as dark stains on that surface, nor in the air above it. Not a single bird wheeled in the sky that morning, on its great wings, or tumbled shrieking before a crevice in the rock. Everything was dead, but he said, "He lives." He pointed.

"See those two massive blocks? That's where I came out. And the chalet," he said, "the chalet must have been a bit lower down, but where exactly? Ah," he said, "it's difficult to find yourself in all that chaos… First you have to get orientated, and it's not easy. Where's north? It's over there, right? So it's where that mound is. We were backed up to a bank of rock, so the stones passed over us and formed that mound. He must be there. Séraphin…"

He shouted, "Séraphin!"

He shouted with all his strength. He cupped his hands around his mouth, pushing out the three syllables with all the force he could muster, so that they made three sequential notes. They seemed to lose themselves, because for a long time you heard nothing more, but then they returned, having collided with the far side of the crater. The name came back once almost intact. It came back a second time muffled and with its angles shaved off. The third time it was nothing but a rustle, as when you trail some light material behind you on the ground.

"We should have brought a gun and let it off," said Antoine.

He said, "But at least you have a pick and a shovel you can lend me…"

VII

Towards evening, little Dsozet reached Aïre. He said, "Yes, he's up there, but…" He tapped his forehead.

"And Dionis and the policeman?"

Because they had set out for Derborence too, that morning.

"Of course," said Dsozet, "they're there too. It was them who sent me."

"They sent you? Why?"

"Because Antoine won't come down. He says he'll only come down with Séraphin…"

"What's he doing?"

Once again, with the tip of his finger, little Dsozet tapped his forehead.

Her heart turned over. She said, "I have to go."

"Are you sure?" said Dsozet. "He's taken a pick and shovel, because he says that Séraphin is under the stones and that he's alive. He says he heard Séraphin calling him. The men went with him, but they came back."

"Why did they come back?"

"They were afraid."

"What were they afraid of?"

"The shepherd."

"What shepherd? Ah! You mean Plan."

"Yes, the one at the Derbonère. He comes down with his sheep, he gets up on a boulder and he says, 'Go no further!'"

They shook their heads: "He knows things, that one."

"He does that, so that when you want to pass, and he shouts, 'No further!' you don't dare go on."

"What about Antoine?"

"Him? He went anyway… Seems there's no danger for him."

They shook their heads.

"Plan says he isn't real."

"Who isn't?"

"Antoine," Dsozet replied. "Plan says he's not flesh and blood, he's a spirit. We can see him, but he's not like us, he's got no body. He says he's come to lure us under, because those ones, they're unhappy and jealous, and they're bored down there."

"What can we do about it?"

But she heard a voice inside herself and the voice said, "Thérèse, go and fetch him."

The voice went on: "Fickle woman, did you tell him what you had to tell him, while there was still time? Did you do all you could to keep him back? Did you stay close to your husband through the darkest hours of the night, the hours that give bad counsel? The cross showed you it was him, or didn't you believe it? Is your memory so short? Have you forgotten that his flesh is your flesh?"

While the men took little Dsozet drinking at Rebord's, though he was barely old enough, the voice continued to speak to her: "Make amends, thoughtless woman: go to him, find the words, find as many as it takes to make him understand, bring him back. Wake him, because he is sleepwalking. Tell him your secret. Tell him, 'Soon we'll be three, there's a little one on the way and he's going to need you.'"

They made Dsozet drink at Rebord's, they said to him, "You'll stay here tonight, and tomorrow we'll decide what to do."

She called her mother who was crying in the kitchen.

"I'm going."

"Where?"

"Up there."

"Oh!" said Philomène. "Oh, Thérèse…"

"Make up a basket, would you? Put a white cloth in it, and two bottles of good wine, and all the ingredients of a good meal, because it's for him, and there can't be much for him to eat up there. Ham, fresh bread… come Mother, it's so the little one will have a father."

She got ready to go, meanwhile, though she wouldn't get far that evening.

The villagers had not yet gone in for the night. They were talking among themselves, forming little groups in front of their doors. They fell quiet when they saw Thérèse. She made her way along the alley where dusk was gathering. A red stain marked an open doorway in which the black silhouette of a head bobbed, or you saw the outline of a shoulder leaning a little forward and to one side. They fell quiet, they wished her a good evening, she returned the greeting.

She went as far as Rebord's.

She climbed the staircase, which was very steep. Her feet made a noise on the steps, but nobody heard it in the saloon above the hubbub of voices. It's not the custom in these parts for women to enter such places, but she didn't go in. She had something else in mind. There was a window there, just before the door, and if you stood on the steps and looked through it, only the very top of your head and your eyes rose above the ledge, which was convenient because it meant that you could see without being seen.

She sees. She sees that he's there. She thought he would be: Nendaz.

He's there with little Dsozet whom they're making drink, though he's not really old enough, and Rebord, and the mayor, and the men from Premier.

She remains there on her step, she calls.

All that can be seen is the top of her head and her eyes. She's outside, in the night, and it's hard to make her out. Her hair is black, her forehead is white, her eyes are black. "Nendaz! Nendaz!" she calls. He doesn't hear her at first, because of the noise and because he has his back to her. Abruptly he turns.

The noise in the saloon collapses, like when one of those stacks of logs, arranged under the eaves to see you through the winter, tumbles to the ground.

"Nendaz, listen, could you come out for a minute?"

They look towards her, but she has gone.

Nendaz gets up, Nendaz leans on his cane, he goes out onto the step, he descends the stairs.

"Nendaz, would you come with me?"

"Where?"

"Up there…"

"What for?"

"To find him…"

"Good god," said Nendaz.

He understands that she'll go whatever he does, and this puts him in an awkward position. You don't let a woman head out alone on the mountain paths, especially not a path like that one, that's lonely, that's dangerous, that never ends.

He scratches behind his ear.

"When?"

"First thing tomorrow."

IX

There were already men in the fields, because the rye had to be brought in. The land tilted to such a degree there that their scythes came up to the feet of the plants above them.

Elsewhere the sheaves were standing upright in threes, leaning against each other and crowned in the middle by their ears. From a distance, in the early morning light, they looked like little women gossiping.

She was with Nendaz and Dsozet, who had joined them to return to Zamperon.

It was misty and still. The air was the colour of ripe corn. The same colour filled the valley that opened up to their left, yawning beneath them though they couldn't see it. From its hidden depths a message reached them nevertheless, a voice that told the same old story, a story without an end and perhaps even without a beginning. It was the Rhone they couldn't see; the Rhone they could hear.

The Rhone that had been there since time immemorial, murmuring, raising its voice at night, letting it fall and die away as the day came up.

She walked fast. Dsozet moved along at a lively pace too, being young, but Nendaz had trouble keeping up, the iron tip of his cane squealing against the stones.

Something pushed her on. You saw her, her basket over her arm. You could see her from quite a distance by now, because the golden vapour that enveloped them (the light mist of summer mornings, or a herald of autumn?) was beginning to clear, though there wasn't a breath of wind and it appeared neither to lift nor to part. Instead it seemed to settle, like a fine powder falling through liquid and coming to rest at the bottom.

She was driven forward. They said nothing, she said nothing. You saw Nendaz leaning on his cane. You saw the high mountains which were beginning to glow in the high air, yielding to its translucence. Then suddenly darkness fell, it was cold and gloomy, as if the year had jumped forward three months.

It was that sabre cut that had fallen across the mountain. The gash was so deep that the sun only penetrated it for a few minutes, when it passed directly overhead.

Thérèse stopped from time to time, to let Nendaz catch up. Little Dsozet walked beside Nendaz. She heard Nendaz say, "How are you?"

"Alright," said little Dsozet.

"That hole in your head?"

"It wasn't a hole, it was a scratch."

"Is it healed?"

"Ages ago!"

Thérèse set off. She heard no more. And once again little Dsozet said to Nendaz, "So?"

"Certainly not, you're too young."

"Couldn't you ask Rebord for me?"

"You wouldn't know what to do with it."

"Ha!"

Love drove her on. She stopped, she set off again. As for Dsozet: "Ha! That's what you think. We've got a gun too, in Premier. It belongs to old Cattagnoud, the soldier. He lets me borrow it when I bring him firewood. I know how to make the flint spark, the only problem is the barrel's bent, so it doesn't work. If Rebord would just lend me his… I know how to pour the powder in, then tamp it down, put in the shot, tamp it down…"

"What about the recoil?" said Nendaz.

"The what?"

"The shock you get in your shoulder when you fire."

"Oh."

"Yes, oh. You fall on your backside, that's what. How old are you?"

"Fourteen."

"Wait 'til you're twenty."

They paused a moment to catch their breath, the three of them sitting on the bank at the side of the path. Thérèse said nothing, having nothing to say, but Dsozet carried on talking.

"It's not fair!"

"What's not fair?"

"I've done you a favour, and when I do Cattagnoud a favour…"

"We'll see."

They set off again.

"I've seen them up on the plateau, they make their nests in between the rocks. They're smart, those marmots… One sits out front keeping watch. When it sees you coming, it whistles…"

He put his fingers in his mouth and whistled.

"They're smart, but I'm smarter. I'd know what to do. I'd hide behind some rocks. I'm quick, see, and light on my feet when I want to be. And I can stay a long time lying on my belly, I can…"

"Yes but with a gun… It's heavy, you know, and long… longer than you."

It was getting lighter. They had come to the stream that starts down in the depths but climbs slowly out of them, until it's level with you. They walked alongside it for a long time, then they saw a chalet. It stood to the right of the path, in a square of meadow dominated by the forest, which was itself dominated by rocks. They went on a little further and a second chalet appeared, then a third, then a fourth, all equally shabby and small.

Love had carried her this far, they were three. Biollaz stood in front of his chalet. Biollaz saw them coming from a long way off.

"So," he said, "you too."

"Where is he?" asked Thérèse.

"I'm sorry for you," said Biollaz. "We think he's lost his mind. Because of Séraphin. He was your uncle, right? Well Antoine's convinced he's alive. He borrowed a pick and shovel and he went off looking for him. We couldn't stop him."

"And you?" she asked.

"We didn't dare."

"Why not?"

"Well…"

"We have to go," she said.

"It's not wise," said Biollaz.

Just then, Dionis and the policeman appeared and came to meet them.

"Nothing to be done," they said. "He insists he can hear his voice."

"Séraphin's voice."

"Where?"

"Under the rocks."

"We have to go and get him," she said.

"You're better off waiting until he gives up," said the policeman. "I have to go back down now. But wait for him here, and when he comes back, you can talk to him."

She pushed on. She shook her head and pushed on. The Donneloye woman came out of her house.

"Dsozet!" she said. "At last! Where did you get to last night? Oh! Thérèse, Madame Thérèse, don't go any further, please, for your sake, stay here with me!"

Thérèse seemed not to hear her. The Donneloye woman called her son: "Dsozet! Dsozet! Come here, I forbid you to go any further!"

She planted herself in the middle of the path, barring his way, so that he was forced to obey her. But Thérèse went on. And Nendaz, Dionis and Biollaz went with her.

They followed the stream, they turned left. And there, oh! She remembered the times she had come before, the beautiful green carpet that greeted you there, teeming with men and beasts: a sight for sore eyes. No longer, because now what presented itself was a massive boulder, then another massive boulder, then a third. Serried ranks of boulders, like the façades of houses, saying, "Go no further!"

The passages between them were narrow and convoluted, alleys filled with shadow into which she would have to insinuate herself, because above the ones in front, higher and further back than them, she could make out the greyish bulk of the rockfall, whose full extent was hidden from view by its elevation.

All of it said, "Stop!"

But Thérèse heard another voice that said, "Go on."

And then he appeared in his enormous greatcoat, with the crook that came up to his shoulder.

He appeared high on a rock to Thérèse's left. He was so still it was as if he stood on a plinth, the only parts of him that moved being his head which stirred beneath his hat, and his white beard.

To the left of Thérèse and the three men, a little above them, there where the ravine of the Derbonère opened out of a pocket onto one end of those depths.

"Halt!" he said. "Who goes there?"

"Ah!" he said. "I see, it's Antoine's wife... Well now, woman, can you be sure that the one you seek is the one you knew?"

He went on: "Their looks fool you. They haven't found peace. They wander about beneath the earth... They're jealous of you, they envy you."

Nendaz, Dionis and Biollaz stopped. She went on.

"Woman," said Plan. "Woman, beware... They appear to be flesh and blood, but there's no substance to them. Come spend a night in my shack on the mountain, if you want to hear them, if you want to see them. I've heard them, I've seen them. They're white, they prowl, they moan, and the sound is like the wind on a rocky ridge, like a pebble rolling along the bed of a stream."

She stopped. He raised his hand.

"Do you know what it's called, up there? Yes, you can see it from here, the ridge with the gash in it... D... E... V... Well he pulled it off, this time."

He nodded.

"As for the one you're searching for, take my word for it, he's as unreal as the others. Only he's more brazen, which is why he ventured down the mountain."

"Don't go," he went on, "because the curse will be on you too. Don't let him lure you in. The fall's shot through with holes, it's full of rocks that are ready to topple. It's all nooks and crannies, twists and turns... Don't go, Thérèse, don't go!"

She said to the men, "Are you coming?"

Nendaz said, "You still want to go?"

He waited.

"In that case, perhaps you had better go on alone."

"Alright," she said, "I will."

X

Coming from the Vaud, it takes seven or eight hours to reach Derborence. You climb against the current of a pretty stream, keeping it company. The churning water between the banks is like a lot of heads and shoulders jostling and urging each other on. With shouts and laughter, calling to each other, like children spilling out of school when the door is too narrow to let them all through.

You leave behind beautiful chalets, long and low, their roofs neatly covered with wooden tiles that have been polished by the rain so that they shine like silver. The fountains throw up jets as thick as your arm, that turn the paddles that churn the butter.

And then, nothing. Nothing but cold air.

Nothing but a breath of winter that caresses your face when you lean over the void, nothing but an enormous hole filled with shadow – that hole where he found himself once again. Could you spy him, down there in the depths?

No, he was far too small.

Six hundred metres below you, he was nothing but a white dot, invisible to the naked eye, lost in the immensity of those wastes, where the rocks, bathed in shadow, appeared bluish and wet, or a forlorn grey with black blotches like those on the face of a corpse.

He was too small to see, and yet all of a sudden the rocks sprang to life, they seemed to dry out, to lighten, to revive for an instant, because the sun had tipped over the crest and fallen on them. He was no bigger than an ant at the foot of those endless drifts.

Still, he swung his pick. After a while he took up the shovel, searching for the one who was no more, for poor Séraphin.

He was no longer in his right mind, which was why he continued to wield the pick in full sunlight. Why, stooping, grabbing the flat shovel by its handle, he set about digging a trench that barely scratched the surface of the black shale. A debris of shale mixed with pebbles against which the iron tool struck occasionally, producing a ringing sound.

She had only to listen for that sound, to guess where it came from, though to begin with she had been lost in the narrow passages that separated the largest blocks at the front, that were more twisted and tangled than the alleyways of a village. Where was she now? In which direction should she turn? She was lucky if she caught a glimpse of sky like a loosened skein of blue wool above her. Where was the south? Where the north? Lost, that is, until the sound of iron striking some hard, resonant matter reached her, saying, "Over here."

He raises his pick and brings it down. He speaks to you from a distance.

She stops, she listens and off she goes again. She circumnavigates one mass of rock, then another. The blocks become smaller, more tightly packed, and at the same time they begin to stack up like a staircase that she now climbs – in these wastes where a woman would never have dared venture alone, except that she isn't alone, because there is love. Love keeps her company and spurs her on.

He lifts his pick with both hands, having removed his jacket and his waistcoat.

He turns his back on Thérèse.

He has not removed his fine white shirt or his new trousers. He is there, he is tiny, because rising up before him is the vast body of the rockslide. And yet he lifts his pick and brings it down, then lifts it again.

She leaps from one slab to the next, from one vast block to its neighbour. He hears nothing, he's making too much noise himself. Then he puts down his pick and takes up his shovel.

Thérèse heard a voice say, "Get closer."

It said, "Keep going, don't be afraid, don't give up. If he runs away, run after him..." She called him, he didn't hear.

And again: "Antoine!"

This time he heard. He turned. He saw her and started shaking his head. He shook it several times as if to say no, no and no again.

She moved forward. He seemed to say something, but she didn't understand. Then he dropped his pick. He turned again, saw her coming and set off at a run, heading straight for the top of the rockfall.

They watched from below. To begin with they saw nothing. They saw rocks. Nendaz, Dionis and Biollaz, that is. Five men, in all, who had come up from Zamperon.

Seeing nothing, they sat down. "What do we do?"

"Nothing. We wait, she'll be back."

"What about him?"

"Oh, him…"

The sun hit them then. They happened to be sitting just where it made a deep indent into a band of shadow. To their right a steeple of shadow protruded far out in front of them; to their left it took the form of the serried teeth of a saw, reflecting the unevenness of the ridge behind which the star traced its arc.

The southern ridge, which was directly behind them.

To the top of the sky it presented its crenellations, its square towers, its gables and pinnacles, so that the sun, when it came, slid into the gaps between them, lengthening towards you, then retreating again.

In front of them and to their right, they saw the little lakes blaze. They had been still and calm, but they were no longer still and calm, thanks to a slight agitation of the surface, as if the sun had dipped a finger in on its way past.

The water, once black, now turned bluer than the sky. It was as if a silver net had been cast over it. Through the mesh you saw a small white cloud leave the bank of one lake, glide like a rowboat over its surface, then appear in the next.

"Well look at that!"

It's Carrupt. He gets up at the same time as he raises his arm.

"See him?"

"Who?"

"Antoine, by Jove!"

"Where?"

"Beyond the big rocks, on the slope, among the smaller ones…"

"Oh yes, I see!"

And the others: "Me too!"

Because of the distance, Antoine was still no more than a speck of white up there, the colour of his trousers merging with the dark patches between the rocks. And yet the tiny white stain of his shirt stood out against the immobile colours of the stone because it was constantly shifting, constantly in motion. Because he moved, you could follow him with your eye. He was moving higher, towards the remote upper reaches of the fall, close to where those walls of rock rose up.

"Where's he going?"

"He's running away."

"God save us," said the men, "he won't be back."

Then they said, "And her?"

"She'll come back," said Nendaz. "What else can she do, if he won't listen to her?"

But at that moment they noticed a brown stain moving a little below the white one. As the latter climbed, so did the former; as the white receded into the distance, the brown followed it.

Had love nodded off? If so, it was awake now.

You saw them clearly in the sun, the pair of them, on that slope that appeared almost smooth from below, almost regular, though in reality, seen from close up, it was a mass of bumps and hollows, shot through with fissures and cavities. He took the lead, she had trouble keeping up, but on she went, for love. Now and then she'd find a boulder blocking her path, angled across it, and she'd have to use her hands and knees to get past it. Or the stones would give way beneath her weight, and she'd be swept backwards as they slid.

"She's doomed if she carries on," they said.

They turned to Nendaz.

"Call her, you know her better than we do."

"It's too far," said Nendaz.

"But... then..."

They didn't know what to say. At that moment, Antoine vanished. A moment later, they lost sight of Thérèse too. The pair had passed behind the upper part of the escarpment.

And there it is: the story of a herdsman who was trapped beneath the rocks, and who returned to the rocks as if he could no longer live without them.

The story of a cowherd who vanished for two months, then reappeared only to disappear again. At the time of writing, his wife has disappeared with him.

They were still there, the five, and behind them, on his plinth, was old Plan. In front of them was nothing but stone and more stone. Nothing lived there, nothing stirred under the sun.

And so it was that one of the men started to whisper, "Could Plan have been right?"

"My god!" the others murmured.

"If it was a man, would he have gone back up?"

"Good god!"

"What if it really was a lost soul, come to fetch her?"

They sat there without moving. The sun, tracing its arc, left them, but the triangle of light had yet to go far. The silhouettes shifted bizarrely across space. The little lakes turned grey again, the colour of zinc sheets.

It was a game that the sun and the shade played in the gaps between the peaks, in the spaces separating one mountain chain from the next, and as another ray of sun fell on their necks, they turned towards it...

They are astonished, and what astonishes them is old Plan, because they see him shrug his shoulders, then shrug them again. Old Plan is looking upwards toward the top of the landslide. Suddenly, turning his head, he makes a gesture with his crook.

They still haven't grasped what's happening when they realise that Plan is going. His flock too. They're leaving.

Turning back, directing their gazes upward again, they see something moving in the rocks. Is it Thérèse up there? It is, and she's bringing him down.

Impossible! Could it be...? It is: there are two of them. A man and a woman.

In front of the five the mountain rises up with its formidable rockfaces and its lofty towers. It is wicked, it is all-powerful, but a slip of a woman stood up to it and won, because she loved, because she dared.

She found the words that needed to be said. She came with her secret. Carrying life inside of her, she went there where there was no life, and brought back that which was living from the midst of that which was dead.

"Hohey!"

They cupped their hands and made the call of the mountains. Their cry returned to them, a reply from on high.

A man's voice, a woman's voice.

It was her and it was him. And now they could see that, when they came to the difficult places, the man helped the woman. Where a rock blocked their passage, he jumped down first, then carried her down in his arms.

At the highest point of the rock wall, the glacier glistened like a honeycomb, but behind those who came, and at the pace that they came, that vast opening in the mountain settled into silence, into coldness and death.

"Hohey!"

Derborence, the word sings softly and sadly in your head as you lean over the void where nothing remains, and you see that nothing remains.

It's winter beneath you, it's the dead season all year round. As far as the eye can see there is nothing but rock, rock and more rock.

For close to two hundred years.

Sometimes, a flock of sheep appears in those lonely places, because of the meagre tufts of grass that push up where the rock lets them through. It roams there for a long time, like the shadow of a cloud.

When it moves, it makes a sound like a heavy shower.

When it grazes, the sound is like the little waves that, on summer evenings, lap the shore rapidly and in quick succession.

The moss, with its slow, patient brushstrokes, has painted the largest of the blocks, in bright green, in grey on grey, in all shades of green. In the cracks between them grow several species of plant and bush, blackberry, hilberry, barberry with its tough leaves and woody fruit, that tinkle gently in the wind like cowbells.

THE END

AFTERWORD

Ramuz's tale is grounded in fact. In 1714, a mountain fell down in the Valais region of Switzerland. An earthquake two years earlier had weakened a large section of rockface beneath the peak of Les Diablerets, whose name means something like 'little devils'. This now detached itself and careered downwards, destroying around fifty chalets that stood in its path. Fourteen people are said to have died, along with large numbers of cattle, goats and sheep. Huge boulders crowded into the head of the Lizerne Valley and kept on rolling, some of them for a kilometre or more. Those that came to rest in streams or small rivers stopped them up, forcing the water to find new paths or form lakes. Another section of the mountain, that had been destabilised by the fall, came down in its turn thirty-five years later. There were no casualties that time, but a new lake was born. It was named like this novel after a non-place: Derborence.

For Ramuz a place is only a place as long as it retains the human element. Derborence, whose name rhymes pleasingly with transhumance, was only ever half a place at best, being inhabited for a few months each year by herders who brought their animals up from lower down in search of fresh grazing. In the story, the soullessness of their surroundings occasionally penetrates their consciousness: "And Séraphin shut up too, at that moment, both of them having become aware of something inhuman expanding around them, something that couldn't be endured for long: silence. The silence of the high mountains, the silence of those human deserts where man appears only fleetingly."

Nothing is always pressing on something, in those deserts, and Ramuz reproduces that tension in his language; in its rhythms. One metre keeps rock time: you hear the glaciers, the Rhone, the scarred and weathered landscape. There is no such thing as a cataclysm in rock time, only seismic forces and evolution, which are indifferent to human suffering. But there's a second metre, and this one is human. It regulates the instant between birth and death. In that instant, a cataclysm occurs: women are widowed, children are orphaned, a village is frozen in its summer state.

"At the time the disaster struck, the air suddenly turned dark, as if day had given way to night," wrote a local priest who climbed up to Derborence two days after the landslide, to exorcise the demons from that place. "The dust that rose up gathered so thickly over the nearby pastures that they had to lead the cattle out of them. In this unprecedented tragedy, God's goodness spared a few persons from violent death so that they could bear witness to His holy justice and His infinite mercy."

There were survivors, in other words, and that fact changes everything. From the moment Antoine Pont's head emerges from the rubble, from the moment he squints reproachfully up at the peaks, Derborence becomes a place again: the backdrop to human frailty, to devils' mischief, and hence to all that is beautiful and tragic in the world. The human instant is extended infinitesimally, just long enough to capture the meaning of life, before the curtain of indifference comes down again.

Printed by BoD™in Norderstedt, Germany